WOLVES' MIDLIFE REUNION

ENCHANTED OVER FORTY

MEG RIPLEY

SHIFTER NATION

Copyright © 2025 by Meg Ripley
www.authormegripley.com

All rights reserved. Printed in the United States of America. No part of this book may be used or reproduced in any manner whatsoever without written permission except in the case of brief quotations embodied in critical articles or reviews.

This book is a work of fiction. Names, characters, businesses, organizations, places, events and incidents either are the product of the author's imagination or are used fictitiously. Any resemblance to actual persons, living or dead, events, or locales is entirely coincidental.

Disclaimer

This book is intended for readers age 18 and over. It contains mature situations and language that may be objectionable to some readers.

CONTENTS

WOLVES' MIDLIFE REUNION

Chapter 1	3
Chapter 2	14
Chapter 3	30
Chapter 4	42
Chapter 5	56
Chapter 6	71
Chapter 7	86
Chapter 8	101
Chapter 9	112
Chapter 10	124
Chapter 11	138
Chapter 12	151
Chapter 13	162
Chapter 14	176
Chapter 15	188
Chapter 16	202
Chapter 17	211
Chapter 18	221
Chapter 19	234
Epilogue	250
Amanda And Lars	259
Also by Meg Ripley	271

WOLVES' MIDLIFE REUNION

1

"Excuse me!"

"How may I help you?" Tina Wright smiled pleasantly at the customer who'd just marched up to the cash register and demanded her attention. Or at least, she hoped she smiled pleasantly. The Crystal Cauldron was full to the brim with customers, and some just didn't know how to wait in line. Tina left the cash register in Nia's hands.

"Yeah, hi. I was wondering if you carry any of those light-up witch hats. You know, the ones with the LEDs on them? My friends and I all want to match!" The woman wore a black t-shirt with 'Basic Witch' emblazoned across the front and was munching on a bag of chocolate balls labeled Eye of Newt.

Tina held back her sigh. The Crystal Cauldron was a serious shop. She carried a wide range of supplies, and throughout the year, her fellow witches often came to her for their stones, palo santo, candles, and incense. It was tourist season, though, when everyone in America descended on Salem and decided they were witches.

"I'm sorry," Tina said, still holding that smile. "I don't have any of those here. You might want to try Ye Olde Broom Shoppe. I believe they carry them."

"Jenny! Hey, Jen!" The woman leaned back and called across the shop to her friend, drawing the attention of several other customers. "We'll have to go somewhere else!"

Tina cleared her throat. Did this woman have a clue how rude she was being? Did she not understand that most of the shops in Salem were run by small business owners, all looking to make a living? Still, she kept smiling. "Is there something else I can interest you in? We have some great books about beginning your journey into witchcraft, as well as some kits that include everything you need to get started." She gestured toward the neatly wrapped packages on a nearby display rack.

Every Halloween season, Tina tried to come up with something new for The Crystal Cauldron. She was proud of her inventory, but she had to cater to a different crowd during the month of October. The beginner witch kits seemed like they would perfectly toe the line between those who were just there to have fun and those who genuinely wanted to explore their innate magical gifts.

"Hmmm..." The woman stuffed another handful of chocolate balls into her mouth as she picked up one of the kits and examined it. "Jenny! Jen! You want one of these?" She waved the kit over her head.

Jenny finally came over to see. "Yeah, that could be fun! We can go back home and show everyone all the spells we learned while we were here!"

Two kits were plopped down on the counter.

Tina rang them up quickly on the second register, which sat under a plastic cover for most of the year. "As that book will tell you, you need to be very careful when you're first starting out on your magical journey. Your energy and intention have a big impact on what you're doing." She slipped the kits into a purple gift bag.

Basic Witch laughed, waving her hand dismissively. "Oh, I'm not worried about it. It's not like it's real, anyway. This is all just for fun. Thanks, though!" She grabbed the bag and headed out the door, undoubtedly on her way to Ye Olde Broom Shoppe for a light-up hat or some cheesy décor.

"Tina?"

Nia still had the cash register well in hand, so Tina turned to Colette. "What's up?"

"Uh, I'm really sorry." Colette held her phone in her hands and chewed her bottom lip. "I completely forgot that I've got band practice tonight. They changed the schedule around. I've got to head out, or I'm going to be late."

"Oh." The shop was packed with tourists. She needed at least three people to run the place when it was like this. "I'm really, really sorry," Colette insisted. "I can message my band director and..."

"Absolutely not." Tina shook her head firmly. "When you started here in high school, I told you I'd work around your school and band schedules. It's even more important now that you're on that scholarship. I don't want you to lose that. Just make sure you go over your schedule for the next few weeks and make sure we're on the same page, okay?"

Colette's shoulders sagged with relief. "Thanks. And again, I'm really sorry."

"We'll hold the fort down." Tina gave her a wink.

"How are we going to do dinner?" Nia asked, turning to Tina as she finished ringing up a large order of soaps, sage bundles, essential oils, and stones.

"Well..." This was always the problem with running a small business. The balance between having enough staff and being able to afford them was a delicate one. "We'll order in. My treat."

"Sweet!" Nia returned to the next customer, smiling brightly. "Hi, there. Did you find everything you needed today?"

The line was long at the counter, extending too close to the door. If new customers came in and saw that, they were likely to turn around and leave. Tina grabbed the next person and led her over to her register. Between the two of them, she managed to reduce the line to just a couple of people.

She was just about to go work the floor, restocking and straightening, when she noticed a customer eyeing the jewelry in the locked glass case adjacent to the cash register. She never wanted anyone to linger too long without being offered assistance. Many people would give up if they couldn't just grab what they needed off the rack. "Is there anything you'd like to see?" She pulled the key off her wrist and unlocked the sliding back door of the case, opening it to let her customer know she was more than willing to help.

"Well, maybe." His muscular arms were leaning on the glass as he looked down inside.

Though she could only see him from this odd angle, Tina noticed the way the display lights highlighted his cheekbones and the long, straight line of his nose. His dark hair was combed carefully back. The scent of his cologne, only reaching her now that she stood right there in front of him, was a tantalizing mix of pine and vetiver. Her wolf reacted with a start, furiously intrigued.

She clenched her hand in the folds of her skirt, telling her wolf to calm the hell down. The guy was probably handsome, but there was no need to go crazy over a customer. Granted, it'd been a while since she'd been on a date. Her work and her coven filled most of her time, and that was a much more satisfying way to live than chasing men on dating apps.

"I'd like to get a necklace for a special someone's birthday. I'm just not sure which one. They're all pretty. What do you think?" He lifted his head to look at her.

Her wolf punched her in the gut as the man's sparkling eyes met hers, and his smile revealed his dimples. This wasn't just a handsome face. It was a familiar one that she'd watched from the sidelines through most of her high school years at Fern Hollow Academy. It was older now, with a few lines and creases that hadn't been there before, but they only added character.

"Dex?" she asked breathlessly. "Dex Heywood?"

"Oh! Tina! It's nice to see you." His smile widened, and he reached across the counter to shake her hand.

She returned the gesture with her left hand, realized it was the wrong one, and quickly switched. Her face burned, and she was vibrating all the way down to her bones. She felt as though everyone in the shop must be staring at them, wondering just what this interaction was all about. Her whole heart and past felt like they were on display. "Nice to see you, too."

"I didn't know you worked here," he said.

"It's worse than that. I own the place." She managed a smile, and this one was far more genuine than the one she reserved for obnoxious customers who didn't take witchcraft seriously.

"Nice. What better place to buy a birthday present from than a shop owned by an old friend?"

Friend. Right. That was all they'd ever managed to be, and even that was tenuous.

Dex wasn't there because he realized how long

it'd been since he'd seen her and wanted to drop by for a visit. He was there because he needed to make a purchase. At least he was going for the quality stuff.

"I'm just a typical helpless guy when it comes to these things," he explained sheepishly.

"Well, let's see." She didn't want to ask who he was buying for and what she liked. She didn't want to see how happy he was when he discussed his mate's or girlfriend's favorite color or what kind of style she had.

Instead, Tina gravitated toward the necklace she liked quite a bit herself. The sterling silver setting was minimal, allowing the stone's beauty to shine through. It flashed under the lights as she removed it from the case and set it on the counter. "This one is pink moonstone."

"Yeah." Dex picked it up, turning it from side to side as he examined it. "That's perfect. I'll take it."

"Would you like it gift wrapped?" She was already pulling a sheet of purple wrapping paper off the roll she kept nearby.

"That'd be great. Thanks."

Tina was grateful that she'd done this so many times. Even with shaking fingers and the feeling that Dex was watching her every move, she perfectly creased all the corners and tied a sparkly bow on top.

She was just slipping it into a gift bag when a little girl ran up to the counter and tackled Dex from behind, wrapping her arms around his leg and hugging him tight.

"Oof!" Dex pretended to fall against the counter before he turned around. "Are you training for the football team again?"

The girl giggled up at him, showing off the big gap where her two front teeth used to be. "No, Daddy! I play soccer!" There was a slight lisp on the last word.

"And she's a star player," Dex said to Tina. He winked and put his finger to his lips before taking the bag off the counter and holding it against his other side, where the little girl wouldn't see it. "This is my daughter, Sage. Sage, this is Tina. She and I went to the Academy together."

Sage gave Tina a shy wave.

"Hi, Sage. You have a very pretty name."

"Thank you." She giggled again.

Tina's heart swelled at the way Dex's strong hand stroked Sage's hair away from her face, an automatic gesture of love and kindness. The love between them was palpable, and it made her forget that the store was full enough to make the fire marshal uncomfortable. The gift must've been for Sage, but that meant Dex must have a mate. He was a missed opportunity, the one that got away, the one she never really had in the first place.

"Speaking of the Academy, did you get your invitation for the reunion?" As soon as Tina asked him, she wished she hadn't. She wasn't entirely sure if she was going to go, and a guy like Dex probably wouldn't do anything so ridiculous. It was just her damn wolf, trying to come up with a reason to keep him there a few minutes longer.

"Oh, I have to," Dex replied. "Debbie told me there was no way she'd let me skip out on it."

Ah, yes. His twin sister, the president of their class. That made sense. "I'm sure it's going to be great. I guess I'll see you there."

"Sounds good. We'll get out of your way and let you get back to your customers."

"Bye!" Sage waggled her fingers again before taking her daddy's hand and walking out of the shop.

Tina watched them go. Her wolf was pounding and kicking inside her, telling her to go after him. It'd been twenty-five years since she'd seen him, and he still affected her just as much as he had before.

Nia's elbow punched into her side and her memories. "Who was *that*?"

"Oh." Tina blinked. The crowd, the tourists, and the fact that they were short a staff member all came rushing back to her. "Just someone I hadn't seen in a long time."

"So, you had to make up for lost time?"

"What do you mean?"

"Come on!" Nia laughed. "You two had your eyes glued to each other."

"No. It was nothing like that."

Because it couldn't be, even though her wolf desperately thought otherwise.

2

"Now, Daddy?"

Dex looked around as they ambled down the path at Salem Woods Highland Park. They'd left the parking lot behind some time ago. It was a rainy day, not the kind that would keep everyone out of the park, but enough to keep most people away. Still, they had to be cautious, no matter how excited she was. "Soon."

"Okay." Sage skipped down the path ahead of him, putting one leg out front and prancing along while her arms bobbed in the air. "I didn't know we were going to the park today, too!"

"It seemed like a good idea to me." There would be no getting her to rest after the huge day they'd already had at the packhouse, and running around in the woods sounded like a good bet. "Did you enjoy your party?"

"Yes!" Sage pranced back to him and put her little hand in his. She held on tightly as she used his strength to pull her up off the path for even bigger skips and hops. "Everybody came!"

"Of course they did. They're crazy about you. Just like I am." He reached over to ruffle her hair.

"No, Daddy!" Sage ducked away and put her hand up protectively. "I like the way Aunt Debbie braided it."

"She did a good job, didn't she?" Dex tweaked the end of the French braid instead, where he wouldn't damage it. He'd done his best to figure out how to style Sage's hair. His own curls were easily tamed by keeping them cut short and combed back, but she liked her hair long and pretty. 'Like a princess,' she'd told him. The hairstyling videos online all made it look easy, but it was still a challenge for him. His twin sister always came to the rescue on important days.

"Can I keep it in for school tomorrow?" Sage asked as she bounced on her toes.

He could just imagine how it would look after Sage had slept on it for the night. The other parents at school drop-off already gave him enough sideways glances, and he didn't need to give them another reason. "I don't think it'll last overnight, but we'll try to do something pretty."

"Okay." She looked around them, even spinning and walking backward for a moment before she looked up. "Now?"

Dex tapped into his wolf senses, knowing that his human eyes and ears wouldn't be able to give him as much information as he truly wanted. He caught the screech of a blue jay and the chattering of a couple of gray squirrels, but there were no humans nearby. "Yes. Let's go over here." He led her off the trail and into the surrounding trees.

As soon as she let go of his hand, Sage was already beginning her transformation. She melted down into her wolf form, dropping forward on all fours as her inner animal took over. Her hands became paws before they even hit the soft leaf litter on the ground. Fur erupted all over her body, and two cute little pointy ears sat atop her head. Her tail was thick and bushy, even if it was still a bit short.

Dex studied her for a moment as she romped, picking up her front paws and then bouncing down on a bug. She snapped at it with her teeth and chased it for a moment. She was changing. Sage no longer had the fuzzy fluff of a young pup. Seemingly overnight, it'd been replaced by a sleeker gray with a bit of white around her muzzle. She was still young, of course, and had plenty of growing to do, but she was starting to look more like a miniature adult than a child.

Sage pounced again, her tail wagging before she bounded back up. She whirled and looked at him expectantly.

"I'm coming," he promised. Dex ran forward, letting his shift come on the move. He felt the deep, satisfying twist of his bones as they changed their formation, accommodating his inner wolf and leaving his human form behind. There was the stinging itch of fur as it took its place, followed quickly by the feel of fresh air blowing through it. His paws hit the ground, and he bumped Sage with his muzzle as he ran past her and then dashed off into the trees.

Daddy! Sage shouted at her father through their telepathic link and took off after him, her little legs pounding against the dirt. *Come back!*

You'll have to catch me! He kept running, moving just quickly enough that she was on his heels. Every now and then, he looked back, just to make sure she was still right there. *You're getting fast!*

Someday, I'm going to beat you! she promised.

He was sure she would, and the feeling both lifted his heart and broke it. She was really growing up so quickly. When she was born, everyone had told him and Marie that the days would go by quickly. After several sleepless nights, Dex had decided that they were completely wrong.

Time proved the opposite, though. Even though some days and nights seemed to drag on until eternity, the weeks and months somehow flew by with far more swiftness. Sage was always a little taller, a little smarter, a little faster, or a little more observant than she'd been the day before. Now, as they ran alongside each other through the woods, the fresh air in their lungs, he became acutely aware of the fact that there was only so much time left with her. Over a decade, yes, and there would be plenty of struggles, but it still wouldn't be enough.

I can't wait until my next birthday party! she told him as she bounded over a twig.

Planning it already? he teased. There he was, reminiscing about her early childhood and feeling wistful over how quickly she was changing, but Sage was already plunging into the future.

I want to go roller skating, Sage said definitively as she increased her speed, still trying to catch up to him.

You don't want to have your party at the packhouse next time?

I want to invite all my friends from school. But we could still have a big cake like we did today! And ice cream! With sprinkles! Sage was getting so excited about her plans that she tripped over one of her front paws. She tumbled forward, rolling head over heels down the slight incline they'd found themselves on.

Dex stopped, holding his thoughts and his breath as he watched her come to a stop. These moments were some of the hardest, when he wanted to rush to her aid and check her over. But as he'd already noticed that day, Sage wasn't a helpless little pup anymore. She'd still need him for a long time, but she could do plenty of things for herself.

Sage quickly pushed herself to her feet. Her eyes looked slightly dazed, and her paws weren't quite steady on the ground. Then she shook out her fur and licked her nose. *Did you hear the part about the sprinkles?*

Yes. Of course. He waited until she took off, then trotted after her. He'd brought her there to run off her sugar high, but sugar was still clearly on her brain. *You've got to have sprinkles. It just wouldn't be a party without them.*

They continued on, pausing every now and then to sniff a tree or the air, exploring the depth of the woods in a way that humans simply couldn't understand. Dex felt a deep sense of satisfaction as they reached the lookout, where they could see the marsh, and they moved along its edge. These were the moments he lived for.

Daddy.

Hm?

Who was that lady you were talking to yesterday? She dodged away from him and wagged her tail, giving him a bratty look.

What lady? The last thing he knew, she'd been going on about sprinkles and trying to decide which kind was the best. This caught him off guard.

The one in the store yesterday, she explained. Even in her telepathic voice, she could speak to him in a tone that indicated he must not be very smart if he couldn't keep up.

Oh.

She meant Tina. That'd been a hell of a surprise. Dex had known he shouldn't go shopping downtown, not so close to Halloween. That was the time of year when it felt like half of America made a pilgrimage to Salem. Parking had been almost impossible, and even just threading his way up and down the sidewalks between the different shops had been more of an adventure than he'd been ready for after a long night at work.

But Sage had wanted to find some very special gifts to give the other kids at her party, even if they were just her cousins and packmates. He'd obliged, and then he'd found himself face-to-face with Tina.

She hadn't changed after all these years. No, that wasn't true. Of course she had. They all had. There were some faint lines at the corners of her eyes, and her curves were more substantial. She also carried herself with a bit more confidence than he was used to seeing on her. Tina was no longer the shy girl with her nose in a book. She was charming and confident, even if she was still just a little goofy.

She was pretty, Sage urged.

Did you think so? Dex hedged. They'd reached the furthest extent they could safely travel before the driving range around the southern end of the park. *It looks like we need to turn around. We're about to run out of woods.*

Sage turned alongside him as they headed back, but she was still watching him closely. *You thought she was pretty, too.*

His daughter was a sweet little thing, but she also had a stubborn streak about a mile wide. Once she had her mind on something, it wasn't easy to distract her. *She's an old friend of mine, someone I knew from school.*

What was her name again?

Tina. Did you have fun while we were shopping yesterday?

Sage was a literal dog with a bone. *You were smiling at her a lot.*

I was happy to see her. It'd been a long time. Almost twenty-five years, to be exact. Having a child made time speed by, but getting the invitation to the reunion had made him realize that it'd already been flying by. How could it have been that long since he'd graduated? How could it have been so many years since…well, he didn't want to think about all of that.

But you went to school with Hayden, and you don't smile at him like that, Sage persisted. She paused, letting Dex go ahead of her so she could nip at the tip of his tail.

He yanked it out of her grasp, flicking it aside as she tried once again. *I never lost touch with Hayden,* he justified. *He and I have kept our friendship going even though we're out of school. It was different with Tina.*

She leaped up, missed his tail, and slammed her

paws into his rump. When Sage hit the ground, her feet didn't quite land, and she stumbled. None of this slowed her down, though. *Because she's pretty?*

Sage didn't understand what a difficult conversation this was for him. Yes, because Tina was pretty. Yes, because it'd been a very long time since he'd seen her. And yes, for some other reasons that Sage wasn't really quite old enough to understand. Tina had made Dex's wolf react so harshly inside him that he'd barely been able to keep control of himself. He hadn't felt that way in such a long time, and for a moment, it'd made him think there was some sort of imminent danger around them. But no, it was just Tina.

That wasn't right. It was never 'just' Tina. He couldn't possibly explain all of that to Sage, though. Not yet.

In fact, Dex had been so dazzled by seeing her again that he'd nearly forgotten why he'd gone into The Crystal Cauldron in the first place. The display of necklaces he'd initially asked about had disappeared when he saw the way her dark hair fell against the side of her face or the way she moved her hands. Tina had done something different with her makeup, too, making her eyes look dark and smoky. If Sage hadn't been with him...

That didn't matter because Sage *had* been with him. Even if she hadn't been physically present, she was his daughter. He had to consider her at every turn.

She seemed nice, too.

Thank goodness. That was a much safer thing to talk about. *Yes, she's always been very nice. She has a neat shop, too. There are a lot of cool things in there.*

Sage had now found a version of skipping that applied to four legs, bounding forward in hops and leaps.

Are we going to go back to her shop? Sage asked. *Do you want to see her again?*

Again, Sage didn't understand exactly what she was asking. The girl was young, but nothing slipped past her. This conversation had quickly convinced him that he'd been right to stay single for the last three years. If he couldn't even smile at a woman unnoticed, then he sure couldn't date.

You know, I've got one last birthday present for you.

Sage stopped, her little ears perky and alert. *You do? I thought I got all my presents at the party!*

Most of them, but I found one more special thing I wanted to give you, he explained. There had been plenty of gifts from the rest of the pack, and Dex had made sure to pick a couple of special things he knew

Sage wanted. Then he'd seen those necklaces in the display case at The Crystal Cauldron and knew he needed one final gift to top it all off.

Sage was alternately lifting and setting down her front paws, trotting in place. *And I can have it now?*

As soon as we get back to the car, he confirmed.

Okay! Sage dashed off through the woods ahead of him.

She had a good enough start that it took him a moment to catch up. Dex listened carefully. They were getting closer to the parking lot. One slip and both of them could be in serious danger. *I think we should probably—*

The pup in front of him instantly flashed back into a little girl. She tripped a little as her center of gravity shifted and she went from four legs to two, but she quickly recovered. Sage lifted her knees high as she ran, reaching out with her hand every now and then to touch the leaves of low-hanging branches.

Dex was starting to think she was getting better than him at shifting back and forth. As he watched her, it was hard to believe that he'd ever been worried about it. Guiding a child through their shifts, and especially in learning how to control them, had been a challenge. All that hard work was paying off now.

He let his wolf go. The animal regretfully slipped back inside to be hidden away for a time. The sound of the woods around him changed as his ears reverted to his human ones. He felt his feet pound the ground, and all the intriguing scents of the woods melded into the general smell of damp earth.

Sage continued to dash forward, not stopping until she slapped both her hands onto the wet hood of the car. "I won!"

He jogged up next to her. "I'd say you did! All that running at soccer practice has been doing you some good, hasn't it?"

"Coach said I'm really fast!" she agreed enthusiastically. "Where's my present?"

"Hop in the front seat." Dex went around to the driver's side and got in. "Why don't you open the glove box and see if there's anything in there?"

"In here?" She pushed herself forward on the seat so she could reach the latch. Sage gasped when she saw the purple wrapping paper and white, glittery bow. "How pretty!"

Sage held the box in her left hand. She tentatively swirled her right pointer finger in the air, just above the bow. The ribbon relaxed, falling through the loops that Tina had so deftly tied, and then fell away from the package entirely. "Yes! It worked! I've been practicing this with my shoe laces."

Dex cleared his throat and shifted in his seat. He glanced around, but the few other cars in the lot were empty. Those little magic tricks had come so easily to Sage that he couldn't stop them, yet he wasn't sure he could encourage them, either.

She ripped off the wrapping paper, opened the box, and gasped again. "Daddy! It's so pretty!"

"You like it!"

"I love it! Can I wear it right now?" Sage carefully pulled the delicate necklace out of the box.

"Sure. Turn around." Dex carefully fastened it around her neck and then pulled her hair free of the chain. "What do you think?"

"I love it! And it's going to match my favorite dress! And my favorite pants!"

Of course it would, because almost her entire wardrobe was pink, but Dex wasn't going to burst her bubble by pointing that out to her. "You know, that's pink moonstone. Your mom's favorite earrings were also pink moonstone."

"Really?" With her thumb and finger, she carefully picked up the pendant. Even on this gloomy day, it flashed in the light.

"Yes, ma'am." He hadn't thought about it in the moment, not until after they'd gotten back from their shopping trip. Dex still had Marie's earrings in a little box, tucked away to be given to Sage when she was old enough not to lose them. It felt like fate that Tina happened to pick out something so perfect, so relevant.

But he had to stop thinking about fate.

"Thank you, Daddy." On her knees in the car seat, Sage launched herself at Dex. She wrapped her arms around him and buried her face in his neck.

He rubbed her back and held her close, enjoying this moment. There was no better feeling in the world than a hug from a child who loves you. "You're welcome, baby."

She sniffled, and something warm dampened his shoulder.

"Sage? What's wrong, honey?" Dex pushed back a little so he could see her face. "I thought you liked the necklace."

"I do," she assured him with hiccupping breaths. "It's just that what you said made me think of Mommy, and I miss her."

"I know, sweetheart." He pulled her back against his chest with one hand, reaching for some leftover fast-food napkins to dry her tears with the other hand. "It's hard not having your Mommy around, huh?"

She nodded against him, no longer caring if she messed up her braid.

"I'm sorry, baby. I'm really sorry." He held her tight as rain began to fall in earnest against the windshield. "I miss her, too."

3

"Don't get me wrong," Kristy said, shuffling a deck of tarot cards as she spoke. Her fingers moved nimbly, pulling out sections of the stack and slipping them back in at a different spot. "I've had readings that've gone poorly before, but this girl absolutely freaked out on me."

"What happened?" Chelsea asked. She held a glass of wine in one hand and had been slowly paging through a vintage book on astrology that Lucille had brought her. Now she looked up, interested.

Kristy sighed, and for once, her hands stilled. "She got up and slapped the cards right off the table. She started yelling at me, asking me who set her up for this."

"Whoa." Jamie looked up from her phone, her eyes wide.

"Set her up?" Amanda echoed.

Kristy separated the deck into two halves and then shuffled them back together as she sucked air in through her teeth. "I guess it was a little too accurate. She told me she didn't believe in tarot right at the beginning of the session, and she was only doing this to make her friend happy. The situations I described to her were a little too on point, and that made her decide her friend had filled me in ahead of time."

Iris laughed as she gently sank her fingertips into her cat's pale orange fur. He closed his eyes and rumbled. "She was hoping to prove herself right, and that you wouldn't know anything!"

"What I do know is that I didn't give her a refund," Kristy asserted. "She tried, but I'd put my time and effort in."

"Good for you," Tina said approvingly. "The customer is always right, until they're wrong."

She enjoyed nights like this at the Artemis Eclipse Sisterhood covenstead. Although they had some planned nights with specific events or rituals, there were also evenings when the sisters gathered simply because they felt the need. They could kick back and relax a little while spending time together. It was in these moments that Tina felt closest to the other coven members, whether they were sisters by blood, shifterhood, or magic.

Kristy shrugged. "I don't want anyone to leave unhappy, but I don't think there would have been any way to please her. Her friend apologized, and they left. I'm glad I won't be back over there for a few weeks."

"You know you're welcome at my place any time," Tina reminded her. Kristy had started her tarot business by setting up in established stores. The Crystal Cauldron had been one of her first stops, but she'd soon expanded to other retailers, events, and even tattoo shops. What had begun as a way to save up for a permanent spot had become lucrative enough that she was content to travel.

"You only like me for my marketing value," Kristy teased, putting her chin in the air. "You know how your foot traffic increases when you can advertise that you've got a tarot reader in the house."

Tina tented her hands over her collarbone in pretended dismay. "What do you mean? I genuinely love having you there. It's not my fault that your gigs make money for both of us!"

As they laughed, Tina noticed her oldest sister,

Chelsea. She was sitting straight-backed in a chair, frowning so hard into a notebook that the two vertical lines between her eyebrows were beginning to deepen. That either meant she was doing research or planning something, both of which she took very seriously.

Tina cleared her throat. "Chelsea, dare I ask what's on your mind?"

Chelsea's head snapped up. She blinked and looked around. "Yes, actually. I'm glad so many of us are here. We need to finalize our plans for Samhain. It's coming up fast, and we haven't even talked about it."

Maeve, the coven's High Priestess, shrugged a little, making her long beaded necklaces clack softly. "There shouldn't be too much to plan. I figured we would keep all of our usual traditions."

"Yes, but those still take planning," Chelsea said. "First of all, we're getting low on candles."

"I can fix that," Tina volunteered. She purchased them in bulk for her shop, which made them more affordable.

Chelsea ticked that off on her list. "Then we need to get a list together of what everyone is bringing to dinner. I don't want to end up with any repeat dishes like we did last year."

"I don't think anyone minded a few extra servings of hazelnut cake," Maeve's sister, Lucille, murmured.

"Everyone text me what dish you want to make, and I'll put a list together," Chelsea instructed. "Next, we just need to hone our guest list."

"Look no further than your own in-laws," Maeve told her. "It's been nice having the Alexanders join us for the last couple of years, and of course, it'll make Kendrick feel that much more comfortable."

Tina pretended to scratch her face so her mother wouldn't see her smile. It was kind of cute how Maeve had found new love with the dragon. It was unexpected, given how much Maeve had grieved for her first mate. Chelsea, Kristy, and Tina hadn't thought their mother would move on to someone else, but they were thrilled that it was Kendrick. He was a dear man and a welcome addition to the covenstead.

"I met a woman at the library last week," Lucille said. "She had a very small coven to begin with, just a handful, but now she's the only one left. I'll see if she can come."

Iris started playing with her long hair. "Would anyone mind if I brought Walt?"

"Are you still dating him?" Jamie asked. "I admit, I wasn't sure if the two of you would last."

"I know he doesn't look it, but he's sweet," Iris said with a little shrug.

"Ah, the proverbial bad boy with a heart of gold," Amanda teased.

"What about you?" Nia poked Tina in the ribs. "You should invite that guy you were talking to at the shop the other day."

"What?" Tina felt every muscle in her body stiffen.

"Oh, a guy?" Kristy asked. She fanned out her cards, holding the deck all in one hand. "Do I need to do a reading?"

"No, that's really not necessary," Tina said hurriedly.

"She's right," Nia said. "With the mushy eyes they were making at each other, I'd say they've already got an idea of what lies in store for them."

"Hold on." Now, even Chelsea had put her notebook and pen down and was leaning forward. "Who was this guy?"

"No one." Tina pressed her fingers to her forehead. So much for a relaxing evening at the covenstead. Even with her eyes closed, she could tell everyone else was staring at her.

"Must be *someone*," Amanda pointed out. "When was the last time we saw Tina getting all flustered over a guy?"

Relenting, Tina brought her hand down and glared at her cousin. "Yeah? When *was* the last time?"

Amanda's eyes went wide. "No!"

"Really?" Chelsea asked.

Kristy clapped her hand over her mouth and nearly dropped her cards. "Are you serious?"

"What is going on?" Iris asked. "Who is this guy?"

"Only Tina's high school crush," Jamie told her. "Dex Heywood."

Nia arched a brow. "You said he was just an old friend you hadn't seen in a long time."

"Well, it's not that far from the truth." Tina gestured at Chelsea. "Do you have any more of that wine?"

"Coming right up," her sister promised with a catlike smile. "Anything to loosen you up and get some details out of you."

"There really aren't any details!" Tina called as Chelsea disappeared into the kitchen.

A few minutes later, with a glass of pinot noir in her hand, Tina took a deep breath. There really wasn't all that much to tell, but they clearly all wanted to hear it. "You can all stop looking at me like vultures, because it's not that exciting," she began. "Dex came into the shop. He made a purchase, we chatted for a few moments, and then he left."

Chelsea scrunched up one eye. "That's it? Come on! Didn't your wolf go bonkers when you saw him?"

"Well, yeah," Tina said, feeling her face flushed. "It always has, but it's not like that matters."

"Why not?" Nia asked.

Tina sighed. "Because we knew back in high school that we were fated. We felt it, and we even talked about it a little. We were just very different people, and we didn't see any way that it could work. Despite what all the teen movies tell you, a jock and a nerd don't make a good couple."

"But what about now?" Kristy asked. "Maybe you guys just met at the wrong point in your lives. It's not like any teenager really knows what they want, anyway. Something could still be there for you guys."

"Nah." Tina looked into her wine glass. The damn pull between them was still there. She couldn't deny that if she wanted to, not after seeing him in the shop. Every cell of her body felt as though it was being magnetized and drawn to him. Her wolf had gone nuts, angry at her for having as much self-control as she did.

"Why not?" Jamie asked. "What could it hurt?"

"He has a daughter." Tina watched as they all reacted to that.

"Hm," Chelsea grunted, twisting up her mouth.

"That doesn't necessarily mean anything," Jamie pointed out. "Things happen."

"Sure, but there's a kid involved," Tina reasoned. "Whatever his relationship situation might be, a kid complicates things."

"Can't deny that," Chelsea murmured.

"I still think you should find a way to see him again," Nia asserted. "There was a spark between you. Maybe it would work out."

"It wouldn't, but considering that the Academy's twenty-five-year class reunion is tomorrow night, I'll probably be seeing him anyway." Tina drained the last of her wine and held out her glass.

"Good timing," Maeve noted. "Samhain is almost upon us. It's the beginning of our spiritual new year, and that brings a lot of opportunities."

"I already said it's not going to work out," Tina grumped.

Her mother rolled her hand gently in the air. "I didn't say it had to be specifically about Dex. There would be all sorts of new opportunities awaiting you at that reunion. You never know what all your old classmates are up to these days."

"What are you going to wear?" Iris asked. "Something sexy?"

"I've got that green dress you can borrow," Kristy suggested.

"Or my black one," Jamie offered.

"I don't know. I'll have to think about it. Chelsea, was there anything else we needed to figure out for Samhain? We should probably get our pumpkins carved soon."

The rest of the coven got the hint, and the conversation turned back to Samhain. Tina got up, went into the kitchen, and found the bottle of wine on the counter. It only had about one serving left.

"Go ahead." Amanda had come in quietly behind her. "I think you might need it."

"Yeah, probably," Tina agreed, pouring the wine into the glass even though she'd considered drinking it straight out of the bottle. "I wish Nia hadn't said anything. I know she meant well, so it's not like I'm mad at her. It's just hard to have to talk to everyone about seeing Dex when I'm not even sure how I feel about it."

"Well, you were pretty young when you two met

each other," Amanda said, leaning on the counter. She had wide brown eyes and a generous smile that made her instantly look friendly most of the time. "You've spent years having to just accept that you wouldn't get to be with your fated mate, and then he shows back up. Any closure you might've had just went flying out the window."

Tina smiled. "That's pretty accurate."

Amanda's eyes lifted to the space just above Tina's head and then drifted around her in a gentle outline. "You're aura's out of balance right now. That makes sense, of course, but I'm here for you if you'd like me to work on it. Could be just what you need right before going to the reunion."

"Yeah, maybe so," Tina agreed. "The reunion is going to be stressful even without having to think about Dex. What would really be helpful is if I could lose ten pounds overnight."

"Don't be silly! You look gorgeous just the way you are, and I'm not just saying that," she added. "You just need to relax and let yourself have a good time."

"Thanks, Amanda." Her cousin had a way of always being there for the rest of them. She was a calming and comforting presence even when the world was pure chaos. "I really appreciate it."

"No problem. Now, I'm going to head back into the other room and make sure Chelsea doesn't start writing out place cards for the dinner table. Her planning skills are great, but we don't have to control every last second of this."

"Have fun with that!" Tina said, lifting her glass.

When Amanda had gone back into the living room, Tina stepped out onto the porch. She didn't bother turning on a light, nor did she need one. She settled into a comfortable wicker chair and looked out into the night.

Amanda had some very good points. She and Dex had just been kids when they'd decided there could be nothing between them. There was attraction, sure, but a true relationship needed more than that.

And now? Well, she couldn't be sure. She didn't know Dex anymore. The one thing she knew for certain was that she couldn't let herself get caught up in him. She'd spent enough time and had cried enough tears in the past. They were now two mature adults who could nod and smile politely and move on with their evenings.

Or, at least, she hoped so.

4

"Why can't I go with you?" Sage protested.

"Honey, we talked about this." Dex sat down on one of the chairs in the entryway of the Heywood packhouse so he could get on his daughter's level. "The reunion is just for the people who went to school there."

"But I want to see them," Sage insisted. "My friend Ella said she got to go to her mom's reunion."

"Yes," he said patiently, "and we talked about that. Ella's mom's reunion was a picnic at the park, and everyone was allowed to bring their families. This one isn't like that."

"But why?" she whined.

His heart ached. Dex knew Sage's stubbornness on this matter was at least in part due to feeling needy. She missed her mother, and no matter how much Dex was there for her, he could never fully compensate for that loss.

"It's kind of like school," he reasoned. "When you go to class, you can't bring anyone with you."

"Oh." She fiddled with the pink moonstone pendant he'd given her. "Okay. But I'll miss you."

"I'll miss you, too, baby." He gave her a hug.

"And in the meantime, you get to play with Grandma!" a friendly voice said off to the left.

He looked up to see his mother walking into the entryway with her arms out.

Sage instantly ran into them. "Grandma! Grandma! Did you see what Daddy got me?" All her sadness forgotten, Sage held out the pendant.

"My goodness," Joyce said, looking closely so that Sage would know she was truly paying attention. "That is gorgeous. Your daddy has good taste."

Sage made a face. "He's not gonna eat it, Grandma."

Dex's mother laughed. "Oh, darling, it's just a phrase. I'll explain it to you over dinner. I just saw Aunt Debbie pull up, so your cousins will be joining us soon. Go on in the kitchen and wash your hands."

"Okay. Bye, Daddy!"

"Bye, honey." When she'd gone through the

swinging door to the kitchen, Dex turned to his mom. "Thanks for keeping an eye on her tonight."

Joyce made a dismissive sound. "As if I could say no to that sweet little face! These grandkids keep me young. Before you go, though, your father wants to talk to you. He's in the den."

"Thanks." Dex heard car doors slamming outside as he made his way down the hall. He turned to the left and into the room that had been his father's den for as long as he could remember. It was a masculine space, with wood-paneled walls and leather upholstered furniture, but Dex knew his mother had some say in the final touches. As their pack Luna, she had her finger in almost everything within the packhouse. The curtains, the soft rug, and the art collection on one wall were probably all thanks to her.

His father was sitting at his desk, frowning at his computer. His skin was tanned and leathery after so many years working on fishing boats. Even as the Alpha of the pack, he'd always maintained a job outside the packhouse to help ensure there was plenty of money coming in to take care of everyone. Dex tended to think of his father as having dark hair, but he realized now that it was almost entirely gray.

"Mom said you wanted to talk to me." Dex

plopped down in the comfy chair across from his father.

"They need to stop updating things all the time," David grumbled. "As soon as I figure out where everything is, they change it."

"Is that what you want help with?" Dex asked. He was no tech support expert, but he knew he could figure it out.

"No, no." David turned away from the computer. He got out of his chair and came around the desk to sit next to Dex, angling his chair a little so that they faced each other. "I actually wanted to talk to you about the reunion tonight. There's a good chance you might run into someone you haven't seen in a long time."

Who had told him about Tina? Dex hadn't even mentioned his run-in to Debbie. Could Sage have spilled the beans? It didn't matter. He wasn't going to make a big deal out of this, and he wouldn't let anyone else, either. "I'm not worried about it."

"I know. You're a grown man now, and the past is the past. If Chris Kelly wants to keep living in his youth, that's his problem. It doesn't mean he won't make it a problem for you, though."

Dex's stomach turned into a lead ball and dropped. He'd gotten so wrapped up in thinking about Tina that he'd forgotten about Chris 'Killer' Kelly over the past few days. "Ugh. Yeah."

"You're well past the point of needing my advice, but the truth is that I'm not done giving it," his father said with a smile. "I hope Chris has matured, but there's a chance he hasn't. If he tries to start anything with you, then just walk away from him."

"No offense, but this is the kind of advice I give Sage about being on the playground," Dex replied.

"I know that, but I also know how much that whole incident hurt you. You had a hard time dealing with it. As a parent, it was scary to watch you go through that. I don't want you to have to go through it again. Just remember that if Chris tries to start a fight, the consequences just aren't worth it."

"Yeah," Dex said quietly. "I know."

"And I'm not above calling his dad," David said, slapping his hands on his knees and standing up. "I don't care if you boys are in your forties or not."

Dex laughed at the idea. "That would be interesting, but hopefully it won't come to that. I'm just going to make my appearance, shake a few hands, and reminisce about old times. I have a feeling Debbie is going to want to stay for a while, though, so we might be late getting back."

"You two should just have the kids spend the

night here," his father reasoned. "They can have a slumber party, and then you and Debbie don't have to worry about anything."

"Well, if you're sure," Dex hesitated. He didn't like being without Sage for a minute longer than he had to, but he also knew how hard it'd be on her if she'd already fallen asleep there and then had to go home and get in bed.

"Absolutely. I want the two of you to have a good time."

When Dex made his way back out to the entryway and found Debbie, it seemed his parents were on the same page. "Mom insisted the kids spend the night," she said. "Far be it from me to say no, if Mom and Dad want to torture themselves like that."

Dex said one last goodbye before he walked out to Debbie's car with her and got in the passenger seat. "It kind of sucks that Tom can't come with you tonight."

"When you're married to a pilot, you get used to it," she reasoned as she fired up the engine. "He could've arranged to be off and come to the reunion with me, but I told him I'd rather he be available for our vacation next month."

"Right. The Wisconsin Dells. I forgot."

"You're welcome to join us." Debbie backed out of the driveway. "You and Sage would have a great time."

"Maybe. I'll think about it." He'd have to see if he could arrange enough time off work, and then, of course, he'd have to pull Sage out of school. There were too many decisions to make around that right now.

Debbie shifted the car back into drive, but she kept her foot on the brake as she looked at Dex. "What is it?"

He couldn't hide anything from her if he tried. When they were children, their minds were remarkably melded. That had changed over the years, as they'd become adults and spent less of their time together, but they could still read each other easily. "Dad was talking to me before we left about running into Chris. I'd given it a little thought when I got the invitation for the reunion, but now..."

"What?" she urged, letting off the brake.

"I don't know how to feel about the whole thing," Dex admitted. "Part of me hopes that he doesn't show up at all, or that if he does, he keeps to himself. I've really tried to put that whole incident behind me, and I don't need it dragged out again."

"And the other part?" Debbie asked. She glanced in the mirror to check her hair.

"The other part wants him to come right up to me so we can get it over with. Whether he wants to talk like a mature adult, or if he wants to try something, it'd be easier not to have to wonder." That, he realized as he said it, was the crux of the situation. Sitting around waiting for something to happen—or potentially not happen—was the worst.

Debbie flicked her hand in the air. "Chris is a loser, and you shouldn't waste your brain space thinking about him."

"I wouldn't have to, if you hadn't insisted that I go to this reunion," he pointed out.

"I couldn't let you just skulk out of this." She rolled to a stop, checked for traffic, and then hit the gas. "You would've made an excuse, and you wouldn't have gone."

"I would not."

"Yes, you would," Debbie insisted, "and don't bother taking it as an insult. It's not that you're afraid to go, really, it's that you're afraid of what might happen if you don't stay."

That caught him off guard. "What do you mean?"

"I mean that ever since Marie's been gone, you've

hardly even given yourself an hour to figure out who you are on your own. You don't go out to bars. You don't go out with your friends. You just work and take care of Sage."

"That's what a dad is supposed to do," he growled, turning to look out the window.

"He also deserves a night to put his feet up or have a little fun. Look, I'll argue with you about your personal life another time. Right now, let's concentrate on Chris." Debbie zipped through traffic. "Even if he bothers showing up, even if he tries something, he's still a loser."

"How do you know that?"

"Some of us still keep in touch with the old crew," she told him pointedly, risking a glance at him before she turned back to traffic. "Apparently, Chris has been divorced a few times and in and out of jail. The only reason he keeps his job in construction is that he works for his uncle, who's a contractor. Anyone else would've tossed him to the curb."

"Loser or not, I'm still not sure how all of this is going to go down." Finding out about Chris's terrible life didn't exactly help, either. It made him just as unpredictable as ever.

"It'll be all right. You and I will be there together, right? We'll be fine." Debbie flicked on her blinker.

They were getting closer to the Academy now, and a knot formed in Dex's stomach. "What about you? Is there anyone you're worried about seeing?"

"Mm, nah. If people think I've gotten too fat or have too many wrinkles, they can kiss my ass. Here we are!" Debbie pulled into the parking lot.

Fern Hollow Academy was just as he remembered it. Some of the trees and bushes in the landscaping had gotten bigger over the years, and the old painted sign out front had been replaced by an electronic one, but it still had the same feeling to it. The big brick building, already old even when they'd attended school there, towered upward. The elaborate cornice under the long roofline and the numerous long, arched windows made it feel imposing and important. They stepped up to the arched entryway.

"I feel like Mrs. Sharp is going to come out and reprimand me for being late," Dex joked.

"Just a few years too late," Debbie replied. "That old bat retired ages ago, though."

The foyer was a throng of people, all rushing to get to the table that'd been set up in the main hallway where they could check in.

"Well, Dex and Debbie!" Serena Wilcox grinned at them as she checked them off her list and handed them name tags. She'd been their class treasurer, voted in for her bright and bubbly attitude that apparently hadn't changed much over the years. "It's so good to see you two! Go on in and have fun, and don't forget to check the silent auction in the cafeteria. This party has taken the last of our funds, so we'll need to raise some more in order to have the next reunion."

"Thanks." Dex took his name tag. He was tempted to put it on his jeans instead of his shirt, which was the kind of thing he would've done back in high school just to be an ass, but he stuck it just above his breast pocket instead. "Well, Serena hasn't changed at all."

"Except that her blonde isn't natural anymore," Debbie told him. "Not that I'm judging. My color isn't exactly what it used to be."

They stepped into the gym, and it was like stepping into a time machine. The large school logo, depicting the mascot of the Fern Hollow Dragons, was still on the wall above the bleachers. Even the old scoreboard was still there. Serena had gone all out with the decorations, decking every square inch of the gym in the school colors of green and black. Top one hundred hits from back in their time were pumping out of huge speakers set up on either side of a DJ booth.

"Well, this is it!" Debbie said, taking a deep breath and smiling. "Isn't it exciting?"

He wished he could feel the same way. Something was making his wolf uneasy. Dex glanced around. There were plenty of people in their early forties, mingling in groups and sipping punch. It was all about as normal as it could be.

"Debbie!" a high-pitched voice cried out.

They turned as three girls swarmed them. Dex recognized Vanessa and the two Jennifers, the trio that Debbie always used to hang out with.

"I'm so glad you made it!" Vanessa said. "Hi, Dex. It's good to see you, too."

Jennifer H. pulled Debbie into a big hug. "Just look at you! You look amazing!"

"Don't hog her!" Jennifer B. said, taking her own turn. "Oh, my gosh. I have so much I have to tell you. I got here early, and let's just say there's already some old drama getting dragged back out. You should *see* what Heidi Watson is wearing!"

Debbie had been squealing and laughing right along with them, and she hurried off with her friends. She paused and looked back. "You should come with us!"

Though he wasn't keen on navigating this event alone, he didn't want to spend it listening to Debbie and her friends screaming and cackling. He'd done enough of that when Debbie used to bring them over for slumber parties. "No, that's okay. You go on."

He moved through the party, pausing to say hello to a few faces he recognized. Clark, who'd had a locker next to Dex, was now working in IT. Jason was married with three kids and another one on the way, and he'd brought his very pregnant wife along with him. Then there was Brad, who'd been the waterboy for the football team but was now a weightlifter and personal trainer. It was strange to see all these familiar faces and how much they'd changed over the years. Dex realized that in his mind, no one had changed at all.

Despite finding a few hands to shake, Dex still felt uneasy. His wolf writhed uncomfortably inside him, and he knew he should've stayed home. He could've been enjoying a nice, quiet evening with Sage, perhaps having a tea party or watching old episodes of *Sesame Street*. He had nothing to be ashamed of as he caught up with his past acquaintances on his life, but he found it tedious after a while.

He was pretending to listen as Jason went on and

on about the birth of his second child when he felt an odd prickling in his back. His wolf was now more on the alert instead of just uncomfortable. Dex rubbed the back of his neck, hoping to ease that irritating feeling. His heart rate went up, and he could feel it pounding in his wrists and temples. He looked down at his drink, wondering if this meant he needed more or less.

Then he looked up again, just past Jason's shoulder. His eyes landed directly on a woman across the room. Her dress was a deep blue, a color that, even from a distance, brought out the dark brown of her eyes. She self-consciously touched her hair, causing the rhinestone bracelet on her wrist to glitter. She smiled and nodded at someone, and that smile made his wolf swirl like a tornado inside him.

It was Tina Wright.

5

"Oh, really? That's awesome." Tina had found Erica Palmer, who'd been her chemistry partner. The two of them had been stuck together in class. Now, feeling just as awkward and alone as she had on the first day of that quarter, Tina had gravitated toward the first person she knew.

"Yeah, I think it's pretty exciting, really." Erica adjusted her glasses. "At least, I think so. Most people don't want to hear about bioengineered plastics unless they're already in the industry, but it's going to make a big impact on our world. I think we should all find it at least somewhat interesting. Anyway, what are you up to?"

Tina accepted the cup of punch that Erica

handed her. "I run a shop downtown, actually. The Crystal Cauldron."

"Oh. I mean, that's great!" Erica had put some enthusiasm in her voice, but she couldn't quite get her face to cooperate with the lie.

"Don't worry," Tina told her. She arched her back slightly, wishing the zipper on her dress didn't itch so much. "I know it's not all that glamorous."

"I was just surprised, that's all. With your grades, I guess I just thought you'd be doing something different," Erica explained.

"I could get through the classes, but that only let me know I didn't want to get into those fields for the rest of my life. I had to figure out what I really wanted to do. Do you remember when Mr. Johnson started offering that entrepreneurial class?" Tina tugged the skirt of her dress down, wishing she'd gone with something a little longer.

"Oh, yeah. I heard he had to teach an extra class as punishment for not properly supervising kids on a school trip. I never knew if that was true or not."

Tina had heard the same rumor, but all that really mattered was how much she enjoyed the class. "For our main project, we had to set up our own small business. It sounded kind of lame, but I actually really liked it. It all kind of solidified for me when I took some marketing classes in college. When I started seriously considering doing this, I found the perfect building. Then I knew I had to do it."

Erica smiled. "You've got to admire someone with true passion."

"Thanks." Tina reached up and adjusted the strap of her dress. She wasn't used to wearing anything remotely formal, and it was making her extremely uncomfortable. It didn't help that her wolf was starting to go batty, as well. It churned inside her, poking at the underside of her skin, growing more insistent by the moment. Fur prickled down her spine, making the zipper feel even more itchy than it had a moment ago. Tina took a deep breath, trying to keep it under control.

Then she turned her head to find Dex heading straight for her.

Erica turned as well, and she arched a brow. "Hey, I remember him. He was on the football team, wasn't he? I always thought he had a thing for you."

Tina had never been close enough to Erica to tell her about her true connection to Dex. "I don't know about that. We're just friends."

"If you say so," Erica shrugged. "I think I see

Bethany. I'm going to go say hi to her." With a wink, she drifted off.

Now Dex had closed in on her. Those brilliant eyes were focused right on her, as though she were the only person in the room. She couldn't even pretend he was looking at someone else, and then when he smiled, she didn't want to.

"Hello," he said as he walked up. "You know, I just can't shake this feeling that I've met you before."

"Is that so?" she asked innocently. It gave her an excuse to study his face. An ancient sculptor couldn't have made a man more handsome. His button-down shirt was a tad too tight in the shoulders, but she didn't mind. "I don't know about that. I don't think I've seen you anywhere before."

"Well, maybe I should lean casually against a locker and pretend that I don't care about anything," he returned, his smile widening. "Or we could figure out which room they're currently using for detention, and I could hang out there. Then maybe you'd recognize me."

"We could do that," she agreed, playing along. "That means I should probably hold a student council meeting or sit in the quietest corner of the library."

They both laughed, and now Tina's wolf was

bugging her in a completely different way. It was active, yes, but far less agitated now that she was talking to him once again.

"Hey, I wanted to thank you for helping with that necklace the other day."

"Did your daughter like it?" As much as she'd enjoyed their little jokes about who they used to be, a simple purchase at her store sounded like a far safer topic.

"She loved it." His eyes got slightly different, but they were soft as velvet. "It made her a bit sad, though."

"Oh, no. Why?" Tina's heart immediately went out to the little girl that she'd met only for a brief moment. "Was there something wrong with it?"

"No, no," he assured her quickly. "It's perfect. It's just that pink moonstone was her mother's favorite."

"Was?" She felt her mouth and her heart twist with compassion. That didn't sound good at all.

"Marie passed away three years ago," Dex explained.

Tina's heart sank into her stomach. "I'm so sorry," she breathed. She couldn't imagine what it would be like for anyone to lose their mate, nor could she fathom what Sage must've gone through at the loss of her mother. "If I had any idea, I would've picked a different necklace."

"Don't worry about it." He glanced at an open table behind them. "Would you like to sit down?"

"Sure." She carried her drink over, surprised when he pulled out a chair for her. "I admit I haven't been keeping up with everyone over the years. I didn't know you…had gotten married." She stumbled over the words, unsure which ones were the right ones. Tina was desperately curious as to Dex's current situation, even if she didn't plan to do anything about it.

He considered this a moment before he answered, his thumb gently rubbing against a bit of condensation on the side of his punch cup. "I think, as you get older, you get to a point of knowing there's a time limit. Marie and I weren't fated, but we got along well enough, and our relationship just sort of happened. We both really wanted to have kids, and we were blessed with Sage."

"She's a lovely little miracle." Tina meant it, too. She was a bit jealous of this mysterious woman who'd managed to get Dex to walk down the aisle when Tina hadn't even gotten to go to prom with him, but she could see how much Dex loved his daughter. That was all that really mattered.

"I think so, too," he agreed. "She can be a handful, though."

"I'm sure my mother would tell you the same thing about me when I was a girl, and probably my sisters, too," Tina laughed. "I haven't been fortunate enough to have kids, but plenty of them are always buzzing around the covenstead. They're all a bit of a handful."

He pulled in a deep breath and moved in his chair, making his knee bump slightly against hers. "You know, running into you again might be very good timing."

"Oh?" That slight bump of his knee was nothing, pure coincidence, yet it'd driven all the air out of her lungs. "Why is that?"

"Well, Sage has some magical abilities," Dex explained. "They've been budding here and there for the past year or so. I was kind of excited at first, because I knew she had to have gotten it from me. I'm the only one in my pack that has any magic, other than my late grandmother. The thing is, I don't practice anymore. I haven't in a long time."

The last sentence was almost quiet enough that she couldn't hear it over the music, but she understood. Everyone had either seen or witnessed the fight between Dex and Chris 'Killer' Kelley. Dex's magic had turned the fight in his favor, but it'd nearly killed Chris in the process. "I can understand."

He pulled in a deep breath. "Anyway, that's left me feeling a bit lost when it comes to Sage. She knows a few little tricks, things that could be dismissed as stage magic if the wrong person saw, but I've been starting to think a lot about what happens as this progresses. If you've got any advice, I'm open to it."

"That's difficult," she admitted, thinking back to her own childhood. "Just like anything else that a kid has to learn, there are rules and techniques. Some of them you can figure out on your own, but I don't think a person could really master their magic without at least some teaching. I was fortunate in that sense. I was completely surrounded by adults who knew and supported magic. If I didn't want to listen to my mother, then my Aunt Lucille or one of the other coven members was there to help me."

"I wish Sage had something like that," he admitted. His head was bent toward hers, and it felt like they were having a secret conversation, even though they were in a room full of people. "My family is great, of course. I rely on them a lot as a single parent, but they don't know how to help with this."

An idea hit her. Tina hesitated for a moment, unsure whether she should say it or not.

"What is it?" Dex asked, as if reading her thoughts. "Like I said, I'm open to advice."

"This could be a little more than that," she said slowly. "How would you feel if I became a mentor of sorts for Sage?"

He blinked. "You would do that?"

"Well, sure." The idea was still new to her, but it felt right. The Artemis Eclipse Sisterhood helped their own, but they also reached out to other shifter witches who didn't have a coven or who needed support. "In fact, the rest of the coven would probably be happy to help, too. Sage might find a lot of people to talk to."

"Wow. That's incredibly generous," he added, his eyes burning into hers now. "It's been so long since we've seen each other, but I can't help but feel like we've picked up right where we left off."

Her heart surged. Where they'd left off had been an awkward point, somewhere between knowing there was a connection between them and not understanding what to do about it. They'd pushed and pulled apart numerous times, always orbiting around each other but never able to get close. "I know what you mean."

Dex put his hand on hers. "It's kind of funny, really. I wasn't looking forward to coming tonight. Debbie convinced me that I had to, but I didn't believe her. I just didn't want to listen to her if I stayed home."

His touch sent electricity shooting up her arm and through her shoulders. Her chest warmed, and her wolf rolled contentedly. "Sisters can be very..."

"Insistent?" he asked.

"Or demanding," she added.

"And annoying."

"Don't forget stubborn."

"But also right about some things," Dex said. "Every now and then, I've thought about you, Tina."

He looked like he was about to say more, but the gym doors flung open. They slammed back against the wall and shivered as a bulky man came striding through them. Two other guys were just behind him, one on each side. The music kept going, but everyone in the gym turned to see what was happening.

"The party can finally start now that Killer Kelly is here!" the newcomer roared, flexing his muscles in his old letterman's jacket.

There were a few cheers, but for the most part, everyone went back to what they'd been doing before Chris Kelly had made his entrance.

"Fuck." Dex slowly turned back around to face Tina. "I was hoping he wouldn't come."

"No way. Are those the same two goons that always used to lurk around him?" Tina asked. "That's kind of sad. I would've hoped John and Jacob might've found something better to do with their lives."

"Or that a grown man wouldn't need a posse to back him up every step of the way," Dex commented. "I guess some things don't change."

"No," she said as she kept an eye on Chris, who surveyed the room and headed their way, his long strides pounding down hard on the gym floor. "They really don't."

"Dex Heywood," Chris sneered.

"Don't," Tina said, turning her hand upward to take his fingers.

"It's all right," he said as he stood up, his hand slipping out of hers. Dex turned. He didn't puff out his chest or strut around. He merely put his hands in his pockets and watched Chris calmly. "Nice to see you again, Chris."

Tina felt her magic tickling the palm of her

hand, building up before she even called for it. She clamped her fingers down tightly over it. This wasn't her fight. She just wished it wasn't Dex's, either.

"Nice to see me?" Chris challenged, widening his bloodshot eyes and tipping his head. It was an old trick he used to use when they were kids, too, an attempt to intimidate. "Is that all you have to say to me?"

Dex nodded casually. "Yeah, pretty much."

"I'm surprised you were willing to show your face here." Chris stepped closer, stabbing his finger hard into Dex's shoulder. "Did you think I'd just let you come back here without kicking your ass?"

"Yeah," John echoed.

Jacob stood with his arms folded across his chest.

Tina barked out a laugh. This kind of bravado looked ridiculous even on teenage boys, much less grown men. Chris was clearly trying a little too hard to put on a show for his former classmates. His blonde hair was a bit too monochromatic, as though he'd dyed it back to its former shade, and the leather was flaking off the sleeves of his jacket.

"I'm just here to enjoy the reunion," Dex said simply. "I think that's what we should all be doing. See you around." He turned back toward his chair.

Chris grabbed him by the shoulder and jerked

him backward. "That's not how this works, *Dexter.*" He spat out his name as though it put a bad taste in his mouth.

Dex swiped Chris's hand away with one quick movement of his wrist. His chin was up, but he hadn't balled his fists yet. "I'm not fighting you, Chris."

"Why?" Chris snarled, grabbing fistfuls of Dex's shirt and yanking him forward. "Are you scared?"

Dex shoved his hands into Chris's chest, pushing him backward. "*Don't* touch me."

Tina's stomach was in knots. Was this really going to happen?

"Gentlemen!" A slim man came rushing over with his finger in the air. Tina recognized him as Mr. Bowman, who'd taken over as principal once Mrs. Sharp had finally retired. "I won't have any of this! We've got extra security tonight, and I'll have the two of you tossed out immediately if I see so much as a single punch."

"Yeah, Heywood," Chris growled, adjusting the collar of his jacket. "I told you to just let old times be."

Dex kept his eyes on Chris. "You won't have any problems from us, sir."

Mr. Bowman didn't look like he believed them,

but he went scurrying off to admonish someone else, anyway.

As soon as he was gone, Chris was in Dex's face again. "I'm not scared of him, and I'm sure as shit not scared of you."

Jacob nudged Chris in the ribs. "Hey, man. Look. Heidi's here, and she's trying to get your attention."

Chris looked, and so did Tina. She easily found Heidi Watson, standing a short distance away. She was still fit and trim, with what appeared to be a few surgical enhancements. There wasn't much to her slinky, bright red dress, which must have been glued on to actually stay in place. She tossed her hair and waggled her fingers at Chris.

Chris looked momentarily conflicted. "This isn't the end of this, Dexter. I might not be able to do it here, but I will find you and we will have a rematch." He took off, strutting like a rooster as he headed over to Heidi.

"Are you all right?" Tina asked as Dexter sat back down.

He ran a hand through his hair and let out a long breath. "Actually, yeah. I knew that was probably going to happen, and I'm glad it's over with. Chris can say whatever he wants to, but I'm not fighting him. Still, I knew I shouldn't have come."

"We don't have to stay," Tina said, hardly believing that she was daring to make the suggestion. "We could go to the diner, just like old days."

"Yeah." He smiled and nodded, looking as though some of the tension from his encounter with Chris was slipping away. "Let's get out of here."

6

"Debbie." Dex tapped his sister's shoulder.

"Hey, look who I ran into!" she said as she turned around. "It's Nick Turlington."

"Hi, Nick." Dex shook his hand too quickly, ready to get out of there. "It's good to see you again."

"Yeah, you too."

Dex extracted himself, pulling his sister aside. "I just wanted to tell you that I'm heading out."

"What? Where are you going? Is this about Chris?" She sighed and shook her head. "I saw his little dog-and-pony show, but that just proves he's still the same old pompous prick. Don't let him ruin your night, okay?"

"It's not that. I, um, I ran into Tina." He hadn't

told Debbie about seeing Tina at her crystal shop, knowing his twin would give him the third degree if she knew. Dex gestured slightly with his head toward the table where Tina was waiting for him.

"Well, now." Debbie's mouth curled into a mischievous smile. "That's a *whole* different matter, isn't it?"

"Don't make a big deal out of it," he told her. "We're just going to the old diner for a bit."

"Sure." She waggled her eyebrows. "Don't worry. The rest of us won't wait up for you."

"Knock it off, Debbie. We're just catching up."

"Hey, I'm just doing my job as a little sister and giving you a hard time," she defended.

"A little sister who's only two minutes younger than me," he retorted with a smile. "I just wanted to let you know I'm leaving."

"Have fun!" she called after him.

He threaded his way back through the crowd to Tina. They got in her car and made the short drive to Peggy Sue's.

"I can't believe this place is still here," Dex said, squinting in the bright lights. He took in the chrome-edged counter and matching barstools sitting atop a checkered floor. "It looks the same, too."

"They made some updates," Tina pointed out as they passed the jukebox. "Looks like they finally went digital."

"Just in time for vinyl to come back," he joked, leading the way to a booth near the back with a framed Andy Warhol print hanging over it. He sank into the seat, noticing how soothing it felt to have her sitting across from him.

"All the best things come back around, right?" she asked, glancing down at the menu.

His wolf surged, wishing a table wasn't separating them. "Absolutely."

"I always felt like I was in an old Archie comic when I came here," she said, pulling up her shoulders a little and absorbing the atmosphere. "I know all the midcentury stuff gets highly romanticized, and I could bore you to pieces with that. But it felt like this was how things were supposed to be."

"This was a way better suggestion than the reunion, that's for sure." If she kept talking about good things coming back around and what was meant to be, Dex wasn't sure how much longer he could keep his wolf in check. Even his human side was a little too excited.

"It was a bit selfish," she said, scrunching her

nose. "I've been craving a burger from Peggy Sue's for about a week, but I've been trying to be good."

"It doesn't look like you've got anything to worry about." His eyes skimmed down to her dress and then quickly back up again. "I mean, you look great."

"Thank you." Her cheeks flushed slightly pink. "You look pretty darn good yourself."

A young waitress came by to take their orders, pausing their conversation for a moment.

"I never thought I'd miss that crabby old woman who used to work here when we were kids," Tina commented. "Do you remember her? All those kids coming here after school had to be keeping the place open, but she always acted like we were annoying the hell out of her."

"Even you?" Dex asked. "I know she was always that way around me and the guys, but we probably *were* annoying. I can't imagine you were."

She considered this for a moment. "Maybe she didn't like the idea of someone reading while they ate. It must not've been the ambience they were going for," she laughed.

"So tell me what the girl who always brought a book to the burger joint has been doing all this time. Have you had your crystal shop for long?"

She fluttered her lids a little, looking flattered that he should ask about her history. "Close to twenty years now, which is almost embarrassing to say. That makes me sound incredibly old."

"No, it doesn't," he countered. She didn't look old. She still sounded like the same smart, quirky Tina. Maybe a little older, technically, but also more confident.

"I enjoy it, though," she told him, twisting one of her rings as she spoke. "I get to support myself by doing what I love, and I feel like I'm part of the community, too. Not that it isn't hard work, but it's worth it. Granted, this time of year is always the hardest, when we're packed with tourists."

Dex watched her mouth and hands, enjoying the way they moved as she spoke. "And then some moron comes in there and takes up all your time asking for help picking out a simple necklace."

"No," she countered. "I'd rather assist with a stone necklace than listen to someone complain that we don't have any wand-shaped glowsticks."

Their burgers and shakes arrived, although Dex had nearly forgotten about them as he'd listened to Tina.

"What about you?" she said, peeking under her

burger bun to make sure the extra pickles were on there. "I didn't ask what you're doing for a living."

"I'm an EMT," he said simply.

"Well, that's quite a job," she said, pausing her burger halfway to her mouth. "I had no idea you were interested in medicine."

"I wasn't back then," he admitted. "I wasn't really sure what I wanted to do at all. I think that fight with Chris was what really did it for me."

He thought back to that fateful night and the sense of complete horror that'd taken over him when he saw how still Chris's body had become. The paramedics had swooped in, acting quickly as the situation was dire.

"I liked the idea of saving people," Dex went on.

"It's got to be hard," Tina said sympathetically, "with the things you have to see."

"It can be." He wouldn't lie about that. Some of the scenes they were called to could be pretty grisly. "I like being the calm and reasonable one in the situation, though. There are these people who are absolutely freaking out over themselves or their loved ones, but I'm the voice and hand of reason. It's kind of a way of taking care of people, and it's pretty satisfying."

"That's incredible, Dex. How long have you been doing that?"

Their conversation continued as they ate, flowing so easily that Dex hardly even remembered emptying his plate. It was just so good to spend time with her, to really talk.

He was just finishing his shake when the waitress returned and slapped their check on the table. "We're getting ready to close in ten minutes, by the way."

"Really?" Tina glanced up at the clock on the wall, surrounded by neon tubes. "I don't know where the time went."

Dex handed over his debit card. "I don't either, but I don't really want it to end. I'm having a good time."

"Me, too." She bit her lower lip for a second. "It doesn't have to end, if you don't want it to. My place isn't all that far. We could hang out there?"

His wolf leaped at the chance, and he dug his fingers into his leg to suppress it. "Sure, if you'd like."

If he'd taken a moment to imagine it, Dex would've thought Tina's apartment would be just like this. Thick rugs dotted the hardwood floors, and a cozy blanket was thrown over the back of the couch. Several plants surrounded the picture window on one end of the living room, suspended in vintage macrame hangers. Crystals and candles were displayed on nearby shelves, along with a lot of old books.

"Nice place," he said as they came in and took off their jackets.

"Thank you. It kind of called to me. The shop did, too. Do you want some tea?"

"Sure."

The apartment had an open floor plan, so the kitchen was just a few steps away. They were soon on the couch, next to each other but also facing each other. It was almost the same position they'd been in at the reunion, like they were drawn together.

"It's great to have you here," she told him, her eyes soft as she set her mug down on the coffee table. "I never thought it would happen, but it's nice."

"It is," he agreed. "Tina, why didn't we ever pursue a relationship when we were younger?"

She shrugged a little, her eyebrows tweaking as she pushed the crocheted throw blanket out of her way. "We ran in completely different circles. We had different friends and different interests. My friends weren't exactly big fans of yours, and I don't think your friends were very keen on me, either."

"They didn't think smart girls were worth the time," he told her, remembering some of the conversations he and the boys had after football practice. "At that age, they just wanted to get in a girl's pants instead of her mind."

She chuckled at that. "I'm sure that's true. I admit that, for a while, I believed a couple who was fated could work through anything. It didn't matter if they liked the same things or not. That didn't seem to be the case with us. Every time we hung out, it was like fate was pushing us together, but the rest of the world was pulling us apart."

"That all seems so stupid to me now. I wish I could go back and talk to my younger self about what really mattered. That was a lot of time wasted." He took her hand, rubbing his thumb along the back of it. Her fingertips were still warm from where she'd held her mug.

She had her head bent as she watched their hands moving together. "We can't really say that. Maybe there were other things we were meant to do. You've got Sage, for example."

"And I wouldn't trade her for the world. You

could be right, or there's another theory I've got." He felt his palms tingling and his wolf slowly rolling, pleased to be so close to her. Alone.

"What's that?"

"Maybe, like you said, we were destined to go do other things for a while, to have other life experiences separate from each other. But then, when I walked up to that display case and you were there, it was like fate had drawn us back together. We knew what we felt for each other when we were younger, but maybe we just weren't ready for it yet."

Her breath was shallow, her lips slightly parted. "And now?"

"Now, I don't want to let myself miss an opportunity because of stupid things like that. I feel just as drawn to you now. More, actually." Dex could feel every part of his body leaning toward her, desiring her, craving her. How had he been strong enough in those earlier years to ever resist such a pull? No, he realized. He hadn't been strong at all. He'd been an idiot. Now, as he looked into her eyes, he finally saw the destiny that'd been waiting for him this whole time.

"Dex?" Her voice trembled.

"Yes?"

"Kiss me."

His hand slipped up her arm, past the delicate rhinestone bracelet on her wrist, and he pulled her toward him as he leaned in. His lips met hers, and instantly his wolf cried out in victory. Her lips were soft, pliable, and sweet, a hint of the honey from her tea still lingering.

Her hand had ended up on his knee, and her fingertips pressed into him as she deepened the kiss. The first touch was cautious, but then the connection between them grew. She began to kiss him with more urgency, more need. A tiny moan escaped her lips as she parted them.

That moan echoed deep within him, and his hands moved to her waist. He traced her luscious curves through the satin of her dress, his tongue slipping into the warm recesses of her mouth.

Tina tipped her head back, bringing him further inside as their tongues twined together. She explored him eagerly, tasting him, taking him in, and then taking over once again.

Dex's head spun as they dove into this new aspect of their fate. His hands roved up her back until he found the top of her zipper. He slid it slowly down her back, letting his other hand follow behind in the zipper's wake so that he could feel her skin inch by inch as it was revealed. His fingers slid down over the clasp of her strapless bra and the gentle ridges of her spine until the zipper stopped just below the waist of her panties.

He loved the velvet of her tongue, but he longed to take in every inch of her. Dex's kisses roved along her jawline to her earlobe, where his tongue played with the rhinestone earring that matched her bracelet. Her perfume was warm and spicy, a musk that smelled of desire.

He dropped kisses down the side of her neck and shoulder, where he pushed aside her dress strap, grazing the bare skin beneath it. With the zipper and strap undone, the top of her dress slipped down to reveal the black lace of her bra. She already drove him wild, but that peek was enough to make him crazy. Dex pushed away the other strap and peeled away the rest of the sapphire blue satin, barely controlling himself enough to keep from tearing the delicate fabric.

Tina's hands were busy, too. She pulled his tie loose and flicked open his shirt buttons one by one. Her hands spread across his chest, her touch sending lightning bolts of electricity through his skin. Her fingers moved up to his shoulders and then down his arms, pushing away the shirt and casting it aside with abandon before she reached for his belt buckle.

Though he hated to put any distance between them, Dex leaned back to take all of her in. His eyes traced up from her bare feet, her shoes discarded on the floor nearby. Her legs were long and supple, soft but strong, and her generous thighs called to him. Her black cotton panties were modest, but as he ran his hands up her thighs, he longed to discover what was beneath them. The curve of her hips was enticing, especially where her body nipped in slightly at the base of her ribs. Then there were the tempting globes of her breasts, just barely contained by that black lace.

Most tempting of all was the look on her face, her eyes soft, her lips slightly parted. She looked just as hungry as his wolf felt.

"What is it?" she asked.

How could he even begin to describe her beauty? "It's everything."

He released her breasts with a snap of his fingers on the bra's clasp. Dex took each of them in his hands, luxuriating in their weight. He brushed his thumbs over her nipples, pleased by the way they hardened at his touch. Dex pulled one into his mouth, licking and sucking, pressing himself against her so that he could feel the touch of their bodies.

Tina tossed her head back as Dex cherished her breasts. Her hands moved along his arms and shoulders and drifted down his back. She wrapped her bare legs around him as his hardness slid against her.

He slipped his fingers inside the waistband of her panties and stripped them down her legs as he slid himself along the length of her body. Dex kissed the insides of her trembling thighs and then the delicate folds between them. He pushed his arms up under her legs and around her hips, keeping her open to him as his tongue traveled further, finding the perfect spot that made her shiver.

Tina writhed at his touch, small moans building as he held her steady, relishing this most sacred part of her body and the way he could make her react. Her thighs tensed. Her hands flung out, and she dug her fingers deep into the cushions. Her hips began to rock, and she took her pleasure as he gave it to her. She cried out, pulsing against his tongue.

Lifting himself from his knees, Dex plunged inside her. She was hot and slick, and the last ripples of pleasure still surged inside her. He buried himself deep within, losing himself completely in his mate.

He rocked against her until he felt her coming to life around him.

The second orgasm took her hard, her body shaking and convulsing, her walls pulling him in further as her cries of ecstasy filled the air.

Dex felt his entire being coalesce at the center of his body and then burst, a cascading explosion that consumed him.

7

"You be good for Tina, okay?"

"I will. I always am," Sage reminded her father. The doll tucked under her arm was wearing a dress that matched her own.

"Of course you are." He kissed her forehead and then looked up at Tina. "I'm just going to get some errands done and stay out of your way. You think about an hour?"

"Yeah, that should be fine." She felt her wolf dragging her toward Dex, but she couldn't act on it right now. Whatever the two of them were, whatever they worked out to be, she wouldn't step on his toes and display her affection for him right in front of Sage.

"I like this," Sage said when Dex had gone. "Your house is so nice."

"I'm glad you think so. Do you want some milk and cookies?" She brought Sage over to the couch, where a tray was perched on the coffee table. The day was gloomy, but gray sunlight came in through the big window.

"Cookies?" Sage bounced up onto the couch. "I thought I was here to learn."

"You are," Tina agreed, leaning in with a conspiratorial smile, "but I don't see why we can't do both!"

Sage giggled. "Chocolate chip cookies are my favorite."

Tina already knew that, because she'd asked Dex. She wanted to make Sage feel as comfortable as possible. Learning magic when tense or worried didn't work very well. "They're one of my favorites, too, but I like oatmeal raisin better."

"Ew!" Sage said with a giggle. "My daddy likes those!"

"Speaking of your daddy, he told you why you were here, right?"

"Uh huh." Sage finished chewing and then swallowed her bite of cookie. "He said you can show me how to do things with my magic."

"That's right." Tina had reconsidered her offer a couple of times. She knew Dex was a gifted witch, especially considering he'd only had a little help from his grandmother. He could probably show Sage quite a bit if he were willing to explore his talents more.

"Why don't you show me what you already know how to do?" Tina suggested.

"Okay. Um." Sage tapped her finger on her lips as she looked around the room. She looked down at her shoes and then back up. "Do you have any shoes that tie?"

"I sure do." Tina fetched one of her sneakers, which she'd slipped off without untying. "How's this?"

"Perfect. Put it right there." When Tina had set it on the floor in front of the couch, Sage bent down and wiggled her finger in the air just above the bow. The laces released themselves, pulling out of the double knot and falling to the side.

"That's very good!" Tina enthused.

Sage beamed at her. "Really?"

"Yes. That was tied pretty tightly, too. Is there anything else you've already figured out?"

"Hmm." Sage looked around again. She squinted her eyes and pushed her finger through the air, making a ballpoint pen fall off the breakfast bar. "Sorry! I'll get that!"

Tina was impressed. "You did a good job."

"But it was just a pen," Sage said, her little brows scrunching up with worry.

This sweet child wanted approval from her, which made Tina all the more eager to teach her. "It doesn't weigh much, and it would take more skill to move something heavier. What I'm impressed with right now is that you picked up after yourself."

"Oh!" Sage put the pen back on the breakfast bar next to Tina's grocery list. "Daddy says we have to pick up after ourselves, otherwise we're leaving the mess for someone else."

"He's right." Tina had immediately gotten the impression that Dex was a good dad. Plenty of single dads pretended to be caring and attentive only to impress others, but she had a good feeling it was genuine with Dex. Her wolf knew him well.

"So, there are several different kinds of magic," Tina told her, hoping she could break this down well enough for a young child to understand. "You can send your energy out into the world to change things, like this."

Tina held out her hand, watching Sage's eyes

widen as a lavender orb of energy formed in her palm.

"Ooh, purple!" Sage breathed. "I want to do that!"

"Eventually, you will. This kind of magic can be very dangerous, because it can damage things. So can the kind of magic that you've been doing. That's why I was so happy to see you pick up the pen. It shows me that you understand there are consequences to anything you do. That's true in life, but it's especially true in magic. You always have to think about what's going to happen if you use your powers. Okay?"

Sage bobbed her head, still fascinated by the purple orb. "Okay."

With a swipe of her fingers, Tina dissipated the sphere. "We should start with what you already know and see how you can improve it. Here. I've got another pen on the coffee table. We know you can knock it to the floor, but let's see if you can push it more slowly."

Tina watched as Sage focused on the pen. Her finger wavered in the air, bobbing back and forth as she fought between using sheer magical strength to move the object and slowing herself down so that it stayed on the table. The pen jerked hard to the right, rolled more slowly as it came to the edge of the table, and stopped with just the cap leaning over the edge.

"That's hard," Sage told her.

Tina nodded. "That's the thing about magic. It looks easy if you watch someone else do it, but that's because they've already been through years of training. What's hard for you now was once hard for me, too."

Sage looked doubtful. "Really?"

"Absolutely. When I was a teenager—so quite a bit older than you—I wanted to use my magic to help me cook. I ended up with spaghetti sauce all down the front of my shirt."

"Oh, no!" Sage giggled.

"Do you know what was worse? I was actually wearing my sister's shirt! She was very mad at me, and I knew after that I had to be more careful with what I was doing."

Sage pointed at the pen. "Do you want me to try that again?"

"Let's try something else." An object that rolled would be particularly hard to control, and Tina wanted to set Sage up for success. She needed to come away from this first lesson feeling like she'd accomplished something, or she'd never come back.

She picked a cookie up off the tray and set it directly on the table. It had a bit more friction to it than the pen. "Try it with this."

"But I'll get crumbs on the floor if I don't do it right!"

Tina shrugged. "Those would be the consequences we talked about. We'll just have to clean them up if need be. Give it a try."

The rest of the hour went by swiftly as Sage practiced with the cookie. It was easier than the pen, but it was still a challenge for her as she shot it back and forth across the table like an edible hockey puck. After several tries, though, Tina could already see that she was improving. Soon, Tina was setting up targets on the table for Sage to aim at. Could she get it to touch the edge of a napkin? Could she get it to the corner or the edge?

They talked and ate more cookies as the lesson went on, and Tina was liking this girl more and more by the minute. It wasn't just that she was cute, although there was no doubt about that. She was also bright and intelligent. She showed her compassion for others by making sure Tina got enough cookies. Her laugh made Tina's heart feel as though it were glowing.

Something about teaching magic to someone so

young gave Tina a deep sense of satisfaction, too, one she hadn't expected. She loved running the store, and nothing would change that. She felt content stocking shelves and managing inventory, and most of the time, she was happy helping customers find what they needed. Teaching Sage, though, allowed her to tap into an inner part of herself. She found the young girl within her who craved knowledge, who wanted to always improve.

Dex's knock on the door startled her. Tina rushed to answer it. "We were enjoying ourselves so much that I didn't even realize it was time for you to come back!"

He gave her that warm smile, the one that made light and heat radiate through her body. It was hard not to think about the night they'd shared right there in her apartment after the reunion. She'd brought him back to her place simply because it was close and they were enjoying themselves, but Tina knew it symbolized more than that. She was accepting him, bringing him in. She was leaving behind the differences that had once been such a big deal. Whether or not that would mean anything in the long run, she had yet to find out.

Dex stepped inside. He looked as though he wanted to kiss Tina, but they both knew better. "I'm glad to hear it. I figured since I didn't get any emergency calls with crying and whining, Sage wasn't being too hard on you," he said with a wink.

"Daddy!" Sage came running to him, wrapping her arms around his leg in a tight hug. "I had so much fun!"

"Did you?" He looked back at Tina. "A good report from both of you. I'm impressed."

"I think you'll be impressed with what she can do," Tina told him proudly. "She's a fast learner, and she listens well. Sage, do you want to show your dad what you learned?"

"Yes! Come here!" She pulled Dex by the hand into the living room and sat him on the couch, then grabbed Tina and put her next to him. Sage went around to the other side of the coffee table.

"We're getting a whole show," Dex commented with a smile.

Sage put her doll on the table. She carefully straightened its tiny dress and yarn hair before she took a step back and held out her hands, palms down.

Tina's mouth tightened. Sage had made fantastic progress for her age and experience, but they hadn't worked with anything as big as the doll yet. They'd stuck to cookies, pens, and a few napkins. She fought the urge to correct Sage and tell her to go back to what she knew. Sage needed the adults in her life to believe in her, and there would be times when she failed, no matter how hard she tried. Still, that didn't make it easy to watch.

Sage's soft brown eyes were focused on the doll. Her fingers were relaxed and slightly curled, but she slowly straightened them. As she did, the doll lifted off the table's surface. Sage lifted her palms slightly now, bringing the doll a couple more inches into the air. When the girl moved her hands to the right, the doll floated along as though on an invisible board. Slowly, carefully, she put the doll back down. Her eyes were alight when she looked up at her father and Tina. "Did you see?"

"I definitely did! What a great job!" Tina turned to look at Dex. "She only did that with a cookie during our lesson."

His face was a storm cloud of emotion. He put on a smile for his daughter, but thunder was in his eyes. "Sage, that was very nice. Why don't you stay here and play with your doll for a minute? Tina and I need to talk."

Something had gone wrong, though Tina didn't know what it was. She stood and led Dex out onto the small balcony that looked over the street. Sliding the glass door shut behind them, she went to the railing. "What is it?"

"Tina, that..." He looked back over his shoulder at Sage and then brought his voice down a notch. It wasn't loud, but it was angry. "That was just the sort of magic that almost killed Chris Kelly."

"I don't know that I entirely agree with you on that," she said carefully.

"No? Because I was there," Dex countered. All the gentleness and warmth she'd noticed when he'd arrived had drained completely away. "I remember what it was like when that fight got out of hand. I remember raising my hands and lifting Chris straight off his feet, sending him higher and higher the more he kept yelling at me. There was nothing he could do about it, and I felt powerful. I just didn't realize how much power I had until I let go."

She could hear and feel the pain in his voice. "Dex, I get it. I know it was hard for you, and it still is. That wasn't the magic's fault, though."

He turned away, shaking his head as he leaned on the rail.

She felt the gap between them increasing once again, their differences getting in the way of any chance of a real connection. Had she been wrong to think they could get past all of that now that they were adults?

Tina wasn't going to give up that easily, though—not on him, and definitely not on Sage. "Magic is about intention and emotional regulation. Yours got out of hand that day, yes, but it doesn't always have to be that way."

"I don't want Sage to go through the same kind of hell I did if she makes a mistake," he growled.

"I don't, either. That's why I think it's important for her to start learning these things now so she can control herself." Tina felt desperation tightening her chest. She'd only had one lesson with Sage and was already looking forward to many more.

Dex rubbed the back of his neck. "Maybe I got ahead of myself. She should probably learn, but it doesn't have to be right now."

"She's already using magic, whether you like it or not," Tina pointed out firmly. "What happens if she goes another year or two without any formal training? What happens when she hits puberty and her hormones start up?"

He still didn't look convinced.

"Do you know what's impressive about her? It's not just that she knows a few tricks. It's that she already seems to understand that she'll have a mess to clean up if things don't go right. At the moment, we're just talking about cookie crumbs or picking up a dropped item, but it's a hell of a start. She's a brilliant girl, and I think she could go a long way."

He let out a long, reluctant sigh. "Yeah. Yeah, you're right. I know you are. It's just tough to see that as a dad. I want to protect her, but someday she's going to be out in the world on her own. She'll have to be able to protect herself. That includes protecting herself *from* herself."

Relief rushed through her. "I agree. I know I'm not her mother, but I only want what's best for her."

He reached over and dared to put his hand on top of hers where it rested on the railing, even though there was a risk that Sage might see. "Thank you, Tina. It's not easy being a parent, especially a single one. You have to make all kinds of choices, day in and day out. With some of those decisions, you won't even know if they're the right ones for years."

"I think you've got a better grasp on it than you give yourself credit for," she told him. "So does that mean the lessons are still on?"

He looked through the glass door. Sage was still practicing, but this time she had her doll sitting on a chair and was trying to levitate a cookie to the doll's mouth. Dex laughed, and that warmth was back. "They definitely are."

"Are you ready to go, kiddo?" Dex asked as they stepped back inside.

Sage was standing at the coffee table with Tina's notebook in her hand. She had her brows scrunched up again, a sure sign that she was thinking hard. "What's Sam-hain?"

"Oh." Tina bit off a giggle at the pronunciation. She heard it plenty of times at The Crystal Cauldron from tourists who didn't know any better, but it was much cuter coming from a little girl. "It might look like Sam-hain, but it's actually pronounced SOW-in," she explained, putting the accent on the first syllable.

When Sage didn't believe Tina, she got the same look Dex did. "Are you sure?"

"I'm sure," Tina promised her. "Samhain is an old Celtic tradition that my coven and many others celebrate every year. We honor the dead and take time to feel grateful for everything we have. It's kind of like our way of doing Halloween."

"And you have a party?" Sage's eyes always gave her away, and they were shining once again.

Tina hadn't quite made up her mind whether or not to take up Nia's advice on inviting Dex to their

Samhain ritual. It felt like a big step, especially since it meant inviting him into her childhood home and letting him meet all the rest of her friends and family.

Suddenly, though, it felt right. It would be a good chance to let Dex get to know who she really was, plus it could only benefit Sage on her magical journey. "Yes. The two of you are more than welcome to come, if you'd like."

"We wouldn't want to intrude," Dex began.

But Sage had already accepted the invitation. "Yes! I want to go! Should I wear my princess dress?"

Tina smiled. "You can wear anything you like that makes you happy."

Dex managed to shoot Tina a look. "Are you sure?"

"Yes, and it's not an intrusion at all. We like to invite people to come and share the celebration with us. I think we could have a good time."

"All right," he relented with a smile. "Then we'll be there."

8

"I'm so excited!" Sage squealed as she skipped up the walkway to the covenstead. "I love parties!"

"It won't be like your birthday party," he reminded her. "This is like a big family party, sort of like Thanksgiving." The hot, heavy dish in his hand proved it. When Dex had understood there was to be a meal, he wanted to make sure he contributed.

Tina had told him at first not to worry about it, but then she'd relented. "Just bring anything that speaks of fall to you. Something a little different than what we usually make might be a nice change."

He'd slow-cooked up a batch of his white chili, bringing along corn chips and shredded cheddar for anyone who wanted to add them.

"It's still a party!" Sage insisted as she skipped up the porch stairs and rang the doorbell.

A woman with grey hair down to her waist and a surprisingly youthful face answered the door. Her eyes lit up when she saw Sage, and she clasped her hands in front of her chest. "You must be Sage!"

"How did you know?" Sage asked, instantly charmed.

"Well, I was told that a beautiful young lady was going to be one of our guests today," the older woman explained. She held out her hand. "That couldn't be anyone but you! My name is Maeve. I'm Tina's mom."

"Tina's...mom?" Sage asked, casting a confused glance at her dad.

"Everyone has parents," Dex reminded her, "just like your grandma is my mom."

"Speaking of, you should come in and meet the other kids." Maeve opened the door wider and gestured them inside. "Corbin! Arden!"

Two boys nearly Sage's age came clamoring into the room. "Corbin, Arden, this is Sage. She's going to be joining us today."

"Aw, she's a girl," Corbin complained. "When you said another kid would be here, I thought it would be a boy. Then we could play cars."

"Corbin!" A woman with curly red hair came marching forward with her hand on her hip. After a second, Dex recognized her as Tina's sister, Chelsea. "Don't be rude. Sage could still play cars if she likes, or maybe the three of you can find something else to play."

"I guess," Corbin reluctantly agreed.

The other boy had dark hair and catlike hazel eyes and was smiling at her. "Do you want to go look at the dessert table?"

"Sure!" Sage followed him toward the other end of the house.

"Don't take any just yet!" Chelsea called after them before turning to Dex. "I'm sorry about Corbin. He's just going through one of those phases."

"It's completely fine."

Maeve held out her hands for the dish. "I'll put that on the table for you."

"Thank you."

Tina appeared then, coming in from another room. "Oh, good! You made it. Where's Sage?"

"Already off making friends, it seems." His heart picked up a few extra beats per minute when he saw her, and his mind instantly flew back to that passionate night at her apartment. He wanted to hold her in his arms again, to trail his lips along the side of her neck, to do a lot of other things that weren't appropriate to think about right now.

Chelsea winked as she nudged her sister with her elbow. "I think Arden has a little crush on Sage."

"Well, that's adorable."

Dex nodded toward the swinging door through which Maeve had disappeared. "Your mother already took my contribution for the meal."

"I told you that you didn't have to bring anything," she reminded him.

"You should try it first, then you can tell me whether or not I should've brought it," he challenged.

Chelsea cleared her throat. "I'm just going to see if Mom needs any help."

Tina shot her sister a look and then gestured for Dex to follow her. "Come on. I'll introduce you to everyone."

The next few minutes were a whirlwind of introductions. He met all of Tina's extended family, including their mates if they had them, as well as several friends of the coven. A whole clan of dragons was present, as well, since Maeve was mated to their retired Alpha and Chelsea was mated to their present one.

Beck, their current Alpha, pulled Dex close as he shook his hand. "Don't let all these women intimidate you. They just want to know you better and protect their own. Not that they can't be kind of scary sometimes."

"I heard that," Chelsea remarked, pinching her mate's butt.

After a while, it was time to eat. Everyone was seated at a massive table in a formal dining room, with every leaf expanding it until the chairs nearly bumped the walls. One seat remained empty to commemorate those who had passed on. Maeve stood and raised a glass of wine. "I want to thank all of you who have joined us for Samhain this year. It's a very important day for us, and it's all the more so when we know we can share it with friends new and old. Blessed Samhain!"

The cheer was echoed through the room, and everyone dug in. Dex watched Sage, who'd been seated at a kids' table off to the side with Corbin and Arden. She was smiling and laughing, and when Kristy came to offer something to the children, she answered politely.

"I think she's enjoying herself." Tina was seated next to him.

"She seems to be very much at home," he agreed.

"But not you," she replied quietly. Tina gently placed her hand on his knee. "It's all right. It's just that I can tell. I know something like this is a lot, and I appreciate you being here with me."

"I wouldn't want to be anywhere else." It was awkward, yes, but he would take that all day long if he were there with Tina. His wolf was so content, sinking into a more relaxed state than it'd been in for years.

"Even when everyone keeps staring at us?" she challenged.

"I've noticed that your sisters are rather interested," he replied. "It's all right. It kind of makes me wish I had something like this growing up."

"What about your pack?" she asked as she passed a casserole dish of baked sweet potatoes.

"We're very close, but it's the magical element I'm referring to right now. I could've really benefitted from a big, welcoming group of witches like this when I was young and learning. My grandma helped me here and there, but she was never in very good health. Otherwise, I was just trying things on my own."

Tina considered the butter tub, shrugged, and slathered some of it on her potato. "Sage will find a lot of support here. We take new witches under our wing all the time."

"Who made this?" A blonde woman down the table was looking around as she tapped on the side of a dish.

It was *his* dish. Dex's mind raced back through the steps, wondering what he'd forgotten.

"I don't know, Lil, but you'd better pass it back over here." This came from a dark-haired man with narrow eyes who was seated across from her. "I need more of it!"

"You'll have to get it from me first, Griffin," Lilith teased. "Seriously, who made this?"

Dex slowly raised his hand.

Lilith pointed the serving spoon at him. "You're coming back next year, and you're bringing this. Actually, no. You're bringing twice as much of this."

"Do you really like it that much?" he asked, incredulous but also a little embarrassed.

"I haven't tried it yet." Kendrick, the older dragon who was Maeve's mate, reached out a hand for it. He put some in a smaller bowl and then raised his brows with approval on his first mouthful. "You've got a talent, young man!"

"Thank you." Dex felt like everyone was staring at him, and he was glad when the conversation turned to wine. He leaned over toward Tina. "I was worried the chili was going to be too spicy."

"They're dragons," she laughed. "I don't think spice affects them the same way."

When everyone was full, Maeve stood once again. "If you would all be so kind, it is time to honor our ancestors."

The party moved to another room. Most of the furniture had been cleared out to make space for the coven and all their guests to stand in a large oval, holding hands. An altar had been set up on one end of the room, filled with candles, crystals, feathers, and even a few bites of food. The lights were turned off, replaced only with more candles around the room.

"At this most blessed time of year," Maeve said, her voice rich and mesmerizing, "when the veil between the worlds is at its thinnest, we honor those we have loved and lost."

Dex held Sage's hand on one side and Tina's on the other as he listened to Maeve's lilting chant. This was the kind of magic he didn't know anything about, the kind that required other people and rituals. It wasn't the same as flicking on a light switch from across the room. He felt honored to be a part of it, but he was also worried.

"So shall it be," Maeve concluded. "We now take time to check in with our loved ones. Please, if you have an offering and a desire, bring it forward."

One by one, the witches moved to the front. Dex watched with interest as Kristy laid something on the altar. She stood for a moment with her head bowed, her lips moving slightly, and then she picked up a mirror that lay in the center of the altar. She gazed at it for a while, then she smiled. Wiping a tear from her eye, she put the mirror down and retreated. As she did, someone else moved forward to do the same thing.

"Can we, Daddy?" Sage whispered.

"I'm not sure." Tina had told them that this would be a part of their Samhain festivities, but he wasn't sure how it all worked. What mattered most to him was that Sage not be disappointed.

"I'll come with you two," Tina said. She waited until someone had left the altar, and then she led the way forward.

At the altar, Dex could see that there was even more there than he'd originally seen. There were photos, flowers, books, tarot cards, and even a piece of ribbon.

"Did you bring an offering?" Tina asked.

Sage looked at Dex expectantly.

He handed her a little bag with a rock and a leaf that Sage had found while they'd been out for a walk together. Tina had told him that Sage could bring anything she wanted, and this was what she'd picked out. Still a little worried, he handed them to her.

Sage carefully laid the leaf on the altar and put the stone in the center of it.

Dex hadn't noticed until now that there was a bit of quartz in the rock, and it glittered in the candlelight.

"Now, you just need to invite anyone from the other side who you might want to contact," Tina directed Sage. "Sometimes we say a few words to help us."

"Like what?" Sage was holding Tina's hand now.

"My mind and my heart are open. I welcome you."

Sage repeated the words. She looked so earnest and so hopeful.

"Now take the mirror," Tina gently instructed. "Look into it, but don't really look at your reflection. Look around it."

Picking up the mirror, Sage held it delicately in her hands. Dex could see now that this was no ordinary mirror. It was a sheet of sheer black, showing only shadowy figures in the dark room. "I don't see anything," Sage said.

"Give it a minute," Tina told her gently. "It can take time, and that's all right."

Indeed, no one in the room seemed to be looking at their watch or even waiting their turn. They all stood back, giving Sage her chance.

Still, he felt his doubt grow once again. How would Sage feel if she didn't see anything? He was truly coming around to the idea of Tina and her coven teaching Sage, but what if she simply wasn't cut out for this kind of magic? His grandmother had never done anything like it. The skeptic in him felt as though it was nothing more than a slumber party trick.

Then a prickling sensation crawled over Dex's skin, and he could swear that the room had become a couple of degrees colder. It wasn't a sense of foreboding, and his wolf wasn't on edge, but something was happening.

Sage gasped.

Dex thought he saw the shiny black surface of the mirror shimmer slightly.

"It's Mommy!" Sage said, leaning closer.

9

Sparks from the bonfire flew up into the night sky, and Tina tipped her head back to watch them drift like little stars into the darkness until they extinguished themselves. She relaxed into her lawn chair, pleased but thoughtful.

Dex slid into the chair next to her. "I don't know how late your gang usually keeps this going, but I have a feeling I'll need the jaws of life to pry her out of here."

Tina laughed. "You're both welcome to stay as late as you want. Some of us will be up most of the night. It might surprise you to know that my mother is usually the last to go to bed."

Dex looked over at Maeve, where she was patiently helping the children put hot dogs and marshmallows on their roasting sticks. It was late, but she still had a big smile on her face. "That actually doesn't surprise me all that much. She looks like she's getting some real energy from this."

"I'm glad you said that." Tina sat forward a little and let her fingers trace gently along his sleeve. "I've got a personal Samhain tradition that I'd like to do before midnight. Will you come with me on a little walk?"

"What about Sage?" he asked.

"She's a kid at the covenstead, which means she's basically family now," Tina explained with a smile. Just for good measure, she caught her coven Sister Erin's sleeve as she walked by. "Since Sage has been hanging out with your little cutie pie, Arden, all night, would you mind keeping an eye on her for a bit?"

"Sure." Erin glanced at Dex and then back at Tina, questions in her eyes but not on her lips. "Not a problem."

Tina led the way across the yard, down a path of paver stones, and through the gate in the fence that surrounded the backyard.

"Where are we going?" Dex asked. He slipped his hand into hers.

She clasped his fingers, glad that they had a

moment to do something so natural. It was hard to be careful in front of Sage, even if it was the right thing to do. "Anywhere our feet take us."

"That's your tradition?" he asked.

"My own personal one, yes," she told him confidently. At one point, she never would've told anyone about this. For non-witches, it was too woo-woo. For truly dedicated witches, it didn't feel woo-woo enough. "It started when I was probably about fourteen or fifteen. I just had the urge to go for a walk in the moonlight, soaking up all the Samhain energy I could. It was always my favorite holiday, and I wanted to carry it around with me all year long."

He smiled as he walked casually along next to her. "That sounds kind of nice. When I wasn't too much older than that, my favorite Halloween pastime was getting drunk under the bleachers with the other jocks. I think yours has a slightly better ring to it."

"I'm sure you wouldn't have thought so at the time," she teased. "I have to wonder how you would've felt about this, as well."

She turned off the sidewalk and into the entrance of a cemetery. The newer stones were large, low hulks of granite, deep shadows against the streetlights that reached this far. Tina moved along the twisting path that went between them, heading deeper and deeper into the graveyard where the older stones stood.

"I don't know," Dex admitted. "I might've been cool with it, especially if I was here with a pretty girl." He squeezed her fingers slightly.

"I like cemeteries all year round, but today feels particularly relevant. Here, you can honor all of the dead, whether you knew them or not." She looked to the left, at a towering limestone marker that was almost as tall as she was. Much of the epitaph had been worn down over time, but a carved hand pointing upwards could still be seen.

"Speaking of, I'm not sure what to think about Sage's experience at the altar." He rubbed the side of his nose with his free hand.

"You worry about her a lot," Tina noted. She'd seen how distressed he looked during the ritual, but she was pretty sure it had nothing to do with meeting so many of her friends and family at once.

"Of course. I have to," he said. "I really wanted the ritual to go well for her. She really respects you, and she was so excited to come tonight. I didn't want her to leave feeling like she hadn't gotten to participate."

Dex sighed as they moved into the oldest part of

the cemetery, where the trees leaned down low over little stumps of stone that could barely be called grave markers anymore. "Then she saw Marie. I don't know what I thought would happen, but it wasn't that."

"Why not?" Tina asked. "I've often seen my father in the mirror. He just smiles at me, or sometimes he gives me a look that tells me to get back on track."

Dex was silent and thoughtful for a long moment. "I was worried about how it might affect her. She's got pictures of Marie, and we talk about her from time to time. I can't imagine what it must've been like for her to see her mother in the mirror like that, but I thought it might be too intense."

"That's understandable." Tina had been a part of these rituals since she was even younger than Sage, so to her, they were familiar and safe. "Kids are often more resilient than we think. Sometimes they're even more resilient than we are."

He laughed. "Yeah, that's true."

He let another extended silence fall between them for a few seconds. "If I'm really honest, I've been worried about how you feel about it."

"Me?" Tina paused as they reached the trees that lined the back of the cemetery.

"I thought it might be uncomfortable for you, since Marie and I had been together. Plus, we were there in front of your whole family," he explained.

"I see." She ducked under a low-hanging branch, leading the way to a wide path that tunneled into a wooded area. "Honestly, I wasn't thinking about it like that at all. Sure, you had a history with her, but she's Sage's mother. I can't possibly get myself hung up on that."

"Good. Then that means I really can come back next year with more white chili," he said with a smile.

"Definitely." She took a deep breath, inhaling the damp, earthy scent of the trees and the ground. "Want to go for a run?"

He eyed her curiously. "You're really not the same girl you were, are you?"

As an answer, she leaned into her shift. Her wolf had been dying to get out for the past week or so, ever since she'd first seen Dex at the shop. It was hard to find time for it, but now it craved fresh air. The feeling of fur bursting through her skin and her bones shifting position was delicious. *Much better.*

Kind of like a good sneeze.

She turned to look at him. Dex was a handsome

wolf, with thick fur, wide shoulders, and intelligent eyes. *Your wolf does you justice.*

He stepped up next to her, letting his shoulder rub against hers. *You wolf up pretty well yourself. I like looking at you in your human form, but I don't mind this, either.*

Well, if you want to keep looking, you'll have to keep up! Tina bolted down the path, her paws flying through the leaf litter. She stretched out her muscles, really letting her inner animal loose. Though she didn't dare lose time by looking back, she could tell that Dex wasn't too far behind her.

You've got the advantage here.

Do I need to slow down? she mocked.

I'd be insulted if you did!

His voice was pleasant in her mind, a reminder that they had a connection that went much deeper than being classmates. They'd known each other since before they were born, when their souls had been split into two. They may have found and lost each other again and again with each reincarnation on this earth, or perhaps there were lifetimes when they never found each other at all. Right now, with the moonlight streaming through the branches that arched over their path, Tina was thrilled to know they'd found each other once again.

The path took a sharp turn to the right. Her paws skidded slightly in the springy pine needles, but she quickly regained her balance. She launched up and over a slight hill, then to the left. A sharp curve in the path told her that their run had almost come to an end, and her wolf began mourning it already. Tina dashed around the curves and into a small clearing where a thick, twisted tree stood at the center.

Dex was right behind her. *Damn. If you can run that fast in this form, I'll bet you do pretty well on two legs. You should've run track or something.*

And hang out with the jocks? Ew. Gross, she retorted. She moved toward the deeper shadows under that central tree. With no small amount of regret, Tina let her wolf go. Her muscles contracted, and her bones pinched slightly as she worked her body back into her everyday form. She panted as she turned her back and leaned against the tree.

He did the same, shifting in a quick flash that let her know he did it regularly. "You're right. You wouldn't have anything in common with someone like that, would you?"

It'd been a lifetime since they'd been in school together, but in some ways, it also felt like yesterday. Her mind fought a constant battle between seeing this handsome man as the kid she knew and the man she was coming to know. "Definitely not."

"I'm sure he wouldn't want to have anything to do with you, either," he said as he stepped up next to her, their feet close in the flat spot of earth among the tree's great roots. "It'd be just like in the movies, where the guy can't tell how hot a girl is just because she's wearing glasses."

She inhaled as he moved a little closer and put his hand on her waist, pulling in the deep, clean smell of his cologne mixed with the scent of the woods around them. "Does that mean she ought to take them off?" She reached up toward her glasses.

Dex stopped her hand halfway there, pulling it back down to her side and threading his fingers through hers. "Definitely not." His eyes were intense, and his throat bobbed as he swallowed.

"Why not?" Her tongue and mouth felt alive with anticipation, a vibrating current that rolled through her body.

"Because she's still the same girl, with or without them. He just had to be smart enough to finally see it." Dex leaned in and kissed her.

Tina relaxed into it, very aware of the way their bodies were pressed together. His arm was strong and steady as it wrapped around her and pulled her even closer. She inhaled deeply as she felt his muscles against her softness, his hardness against her curves.

She opened up to him, her lips parting and their tongues twining. He spread his fingers as he ran a hand along her lower back, curling them in to relish in the curve of her hip. Dex still had her right hand captured, but she lifted her left one up and over his shoulder, skimming her fingertips through the short, freshly cut hairs on the back of his neck.

The passion she felt was even stronger than the Samhain energy she pulled in from these walks. She was with her mate, connected, entwined. There was a certain magic in being completely alone, without any judgment or worry, only the trees to sigh in the late-night breeze around them. Anything could happen right now, but being with Dex already felt like a miracle.

A beeping sound cut into the air around them. Dex jumped back and grabbed his phone. "I'm sorry. That's the notification sound for work."

She waited, breathless from his kiss, as he checked his phone.

He groaned. "I'm sorry. I just got called in. I guess the streets are still rampant with tourists who want to have a particularly memorable time while they're here."

Tina pushed away from the tree, just now realizing how much the bark had been digging into her back. She'd been a little too distracted a moment ago. "Then I guess we'd better head back."

"Listen, I really am sorry." He caught her arm as they moved through the little clearing. The moonlight was just enough to illuminate his face and let her see how very sincere he was. "If I had any choice…"

"No," she insisted with a smile. "That's just life. Besides, it just means we'll need to find time together sometime soon."

He let out a frustrated sigh. "We can definitely agree on that."

"I assume you need to get to work as soon as possible?" she asked as they reached the path once again.

His shoulders slumped a little. "Yeah, they need me."

"Then I'll race you!" Tina bolted forward, unleashing her wolf again as she ran. She went into the air from two feet and landed on four, flying as fast as she could.

You just keep surprising me, don't you?

I do my best! The faster they went, the sooner she'd have to say goodbye to him for the night, yet she couldn't hold herself back. Tina felt light and free, and not simply because her wolf was getting so much exercise.

Dex caught up to her this time, his paws pounding the ground right next to hers. This wasn't the hot jock who'd caught her eye in study hall and made her wolf swoon. Some of that was still there inside him, and his looks had really only improved over time, but there was a lot more to Dexter Heywood now than there'd ever been when they were kids. He was kind and caring. He loved his daughter and would do anything for her. She was pleasantly surprised to find that he was also rather intelligent, something she'd never ascribed to all the football bros who only seemed interested in throwing around a pigskin and eating as much as they possibly could.

It was easy enough to fall for a hot guy, but there was so much more to him now.

10

"Damn!" Adrian hit the brakes and then the horn. "You'd think all the lights and sirens would be enough to make people get out of the way."

Dex held on tight as they navigated Salem's narrowest streets. "Easy there. We don't want to have to call another ambulance to take care of us."

Adrian shook his head as he took a hard left.

"I'm just messing with you. I'd much rather have you drive than Lester, anyway."

"Man, don't make me laugh when I'm supposed to be concentrating!" Adrian replied, laughing anyway. "I don't know how they've kept him on so long."

"He's a little slow," Dex admitted, "but he really knows what he's doing. I think it calms people down a little when they see that a grandpa is taking care of them. There's not as much urgency around the situation."

"Well, let's see how much urgency is waiting for us here." Adrian pulled up at the scene.

They were the first to arrive. Dex hopped out of the ambulance and assessed the area, their flashing lights illuminating it in the dark. A black coupe with rental plates had its bumper kissing a fire hydrant, tipping it just far enough without shooting a column of water into the air. A couple stood next to it, arguing.

The woman slapped the man with her purse. "You're such a fucking idiot! I told you that you couldn't drive!"

The man put his hands up to protect himself and staggered backward. "It's not my fault, Sheila! It's not my fault! That guy came out of nowhere."

Dex and Adrian shared a look. This was going to be interesting.

"Is anyone injured?" Dex raised his voice to make sure the couple could hear them over their fighting.

Sheila turned to him with wide, startled eyes. "Huh? Oh. Just that guy over there." She gestured toward a grassy area between two buildings.

"I've got the lovebirds," Adrian told him.

Dex hurried over to the grass. A man lay on his back with his crumpled bicycle next to him.

"Sir, can you hear me? I'm with the ambulance service. I'm here to help." Dex knelt next to the man, putting his bag nearby.

"They hit me," the man groaned.

"Looks like you were wearing your helmet, at least." Dex grabbed his penlight and checked the man's eyes. No sign of a concussion, but with the bicycle being that mangled, he knew there had to be injuries somewhere. "Can you tell me where it hurts?"

"Here." His hands had been flung over his head, but now he brought one down and touched his side.

The fabric of his shirt was soaked with blood, and when Dex lifted it, he could see why. The soft flesh of the man's belly had been ripped open. Whether it was from the initial impact or falling, he couldn't tell. Either way, the injury was near some major arteries.

"Can you tell me your name?" Dex quickly began taking his other vitals. The heartbeat was light and thready.

"Wayne. Wayne Cunningham."

"It's nice to meet you, Wayne." Dex opened his

bag to take a few other vitals. "Did you have anything to drink tonight?"

"No," he gasped. "I was on my way home from work. This time of year, I don't bother driving. You can't get through with all the damn tourists."

Dex snorted. "That's for damn sure."

"I had the right of way, but that car just came out of nowhere and hit me."

"Must've been pretty hard, too." Dex went back to examining the wound. It was deep, ragged, and bleeding profusely.

"I feel dizzy. I'm scared," Wayne said.

He had every right to be. "Don't worry. We're going to get you to the hospital and get you fixed up. I'm just going to put some bandages on to stop the bleeding. You might feel some pressure, okay?"

"Okay." His voice sounded even more feeble.

Dex knew what he had to do. This wasn't the first time, but he had to be careful. If he used his talent too much, someone would figure it out. Well, they'd figure out something was weird, anyway. Dex took several big gauze bandages from his bag and laid them gently over the wound. He put his gloved hand over them, pulled in a deep breath, and closed his eyes.

This was the one bit of magic he'd allowed

himself in all these years. Nothing else. Dex pushed healing energy out of his hand, imagining a cool blue light enveloping the wound. He thought about platelets clotting the blood, about new skin growing together, about keeping Wayne alive. Not too much. Just enough. Just enough to get him to the hospital, where the pros could work the real magic.

He pulled his hand back as he heard the rattling wheels of the gurney on the brick streets.

"Police are here," Adrian informed him. "They're handling the rest of the mess, but it looked like you could use this."

"Thanks. Abdominal wound with severe bleeding. Says the car hit him."

"You don't believe me?" Wayne asked pitifully.

He was old enough that he could be Dex's father, and Dex truly felt sorry for him. "I believe you, sir. I was just reporting to my colleague here." It wasn't his job to make judgments on who was at fault or who hit who, but Wayne didn't need that kind of explanation right now.

They got him safely onto the gurney and into the ambulance.

"Will you stay with me?" Wayne asked him.

Adrian heard the request and instantly went to get behind the wheel.

"I'm right here, Wayne. Don't worry. We've got the best driver in the business getting you to the hospital." The sirens went on just then, and the ambulance moved beneath them.

Wayne smiled at Dex. His eyes were pale and watery, and Dex realized he might have been even older than he'd initially thought. "You remind me of my son, you know."

"Tell me about him." Dex continued to monitor the man's vitals. He was in poor condition, but he was going to make it.

"He lives all the way in California. Went out there just for college, but he never came back. You know how it is. He met a girl, got married. They've got kids now and a new life. I miss them, but I'm proud. How about you? Do you have any kids?"

Talking usually comforted the patients, even if it was only because it was such a good distraction. "A little girl. She's seven."

"How darling." Apparently, Wayne didn't need to see her to think so. He was old enough to feel that any child was adorable and precious. "You and your wife are very lucky."

Dex choked back his reply. "We are. Thank you."

They arrived at the hospital soon afterward. Dex unloaded the gurney and wheeled Wayne inside.

"They're going to take good care of you, Wayne. You heal up, and you watch out for those damn tourists, okay?"

The old man smiled at him. "You're a good boy."

Nurses swarmed around the gurney, taking Wayne's information from Dex and then assessing the patient for themselves. They called back and forth as they rushed him down the hall, ordering tests and procedures. Dex watched them go. They would take care of Wayne, of course, but part of him wishes that he could stay with the old man a little longer.

The rest of his shift was relatively quiet. He and Adrian showed up at another car accident, but no one was injured beyond a couple of bruises. At another call, a wheelchair bound man had fallen to the floor and his frail wife had been unable to get him up by herself.

When he clocked out, dawn was creeping up on the horizon. It spread slowly over the sky, dispersing any late-night revelers and calling out those who had mundane jobs to get to.

"Go home and get some sleep," Adrian advised. "You look like you could use it."

"I'll try, but I'm not making any promises." Dex drove to the packhouse. He was lucky to have a place where he could always bring Sage, no matter what the circumstances, and know that she was cared for. With his job and no spouse, he needed that support far more than he ever thought he would. Every day, he saw plenty of people who didn't have that kind of support, and he didn't know how they made it.

"Good morning!" Debbie chirped when he let himself in the back door just off the kitchen.

"If you say it is." The smell of fresh coffee lured him over the rack of mismatched mugs, a collection that his mother had built over the years. He picked one with a cat on it. The tail made up the handle, and it'd always amused him as a kid. He could use a bit of amusement right now.

"I do say," Debbie replied as she cracked a couple of eggs into a bowl. "I got up early and had a good workout, so I'm ready for the day. Do you want some eggs?"

"I hate to ask, but I wouldn't turn them down." He filled his mug and then put a bagel in the toaster. Dex checked his watch. "I think I've got just enough time to eat before I have to wake up Sage and get her ready for school."

"Good luck with that. I heard she was pretty wound up when you dropped her off, all excited about the Samhain party with Tina's family." Debbie looked up at him as she scrambled the eggs with a fork. "It sounds like the two of you are getting pretty cozy."

"I guess. I don't know what to call it." He took a long sip of his coffee. "Damn, that's strong."

"Just how I like it. And why don't you know? The two of you are fated. There's not much to think about," Debbie reasoned as she poured the eggs into the pan, watching them sizzle for a moment before she stirred them with a spatula.

He turned to the fridge, digging around until he found some cream cheese. "If I only had myself to consider, then sure. Whatever."

"Whatever?" his twin echoed. "How romantic. I'll bet she just goes wild when you talk like that."

"Come on. You know what I mean."

"I'm not sure I do." She pushed the eggs around a little more as she seasoned them.

"I've got to think about Sage."

"You already are." Debbie left the eggs to toast a little in the pan while she poured herself a cup of coffee and got a muffin from the box on the counter. "In fact, she's about the only thing you do think about."

"That's not true." The bagel popped up. He grabbed each piece with his fingertips and flicked them onto a plate, not wanting to bother with tongs.

"Okay, work and Sage," Debbie amended, "but that's it."

"Maybe a little bit of football?" Dex joked as he brought his meal to the table.

She sat down across from him. Debbie had picked one of her favorite childhood mugs as well, showing a silhouette of a little red devil and reading, 'The Devil Made Me Do It.' "Fine. A little. But take it from me: being a parent is really hard. It's easy to get lost in your kids and completely forget who you are as a person. You deserve a few things for yourself."

"Sure, but we're talking about bringing a whole new person into Sage's life," he countered. "I have to be careful."

Debbie took a bite of her eggs and then pointed her fork at him. "Haven't you already brought Tina into Sage's life?"

"Technically, yes, but Sage doesn't know there's anything between Tina and me." Dex slathered the cream cheese onto his bagel. It wasn't exactly healthy, but he was too tired and worn out to care.

"She knows more than you think. Kids always do," Debbie cautioned.

He couldn't completely argue with that. Sage had

certainly noticed the chemistry between Dex and Tina when they'd encountered each other at the shop, but Dex had been careful not to be too obvious. "Regardless of how I feel about Tina, Sage needs someone who can help her with her magic."

Debbie studied him for a long moment. "You're not good enough?"

"You know it's not the same," he sighed.

"That's right, because you refuse to explore that part of yourself," she retorted. Debbie had never beat around the bush with him. It was both annoying and refreshing.

Dex knew she was waiting for him to justify his avoidance of magic as he always did, citing the fight with Chris. He watched her face as he gave her a completely different answer. "Actually, I used magic just a few hours ago."

She'd been in the middle of a drink. Debbie choked on her coffee, splattering it on the table. She grabbed her napkin and put it over her face. "Damn, dude! You made it come out of my nose!"

He laughed as she hurried back over to the sink to clean herself up.

"Okay, let's try that again." Debbie resumed her seat and folded her hands carefully in front of her, being sure not to touch her food. "You did what, now?"

"It was while I was on a call." He told her about Wayne, how pitiful and scared the poor old man was. "There's only so much I can do to patch someone up, and this guy just wasn't going to make it. The people who hurt him didn't give a shit, and they may not have even called the accident in right away. I couldn't let him lie there."

Debbie still wasn't eating, but now it was because she was listening so intently. "So you healed him?"

"No," he quickly corrected. "As much as I'd like to, I'd never get away with that. I just sort of patched him up a little, enough to make sure he could live long enough to get proper stitches."

"Dex!" She flung her hands in the air in frustration. "I didn't know you could do that! And I'm your twin! What the hell?"

"It's not something I've always known how to do." He went back to his food, mostly because he knew he'd need the fuel to get through the rest of the day. "My work is what influenced me the most to try it."

"So you've done this before?"

"Just a few times, when it's a situation like this." He finished off the last bite of eggs.

"I don't get you. Aren't you proud?"

He considered this. In fact, he'd considered it every time it happened, but he never quite came to a solid conclusion. "Yes, in a way, but I also feel extremely guilty. I know my magic has hurt someone, and I can tell myself that I'm making up for it by healing others. It still doesn't feel quite right, though. It's weird."

Debbie bit into the top of her muffin. "I'm guessing that these lessons Sage is getting from Tina are getting you interested in magic again."

"A little. I think I also feel guilty that I'm letting someone else teach Sage because I don't feel like I know enough. I don't know, Deb. It just feels like an impossible situation." He braced his forehead on his palm, ready to get Sage off to school so he could take a shower and get to sleep.

"Welcome to parenthood. It's the ultimate impossible situation." Debbie reached across the table and grabbed his hand. "Hey, you're being way too hard on yourself. You always have been, and you need to stop."

"You don't understand—"

"You're right, I don't," she said firmly. "You and I don't just have the same parents. We shared the same womb. We're as close as two people can be, yet

I wasn't born with the same gift you were. I don't get it, but I'm incredibly jealous. I always have been."

"Really?"

"Hell, yes. And I think you should start giving yourself some grace about the whole thing. You didn't ask to have that power, and most of the people around you didn't know how to help you with it. You're doing everything for Sage to make sure she has a better chance at controlling her magic and figuring out how to use it in her life, which makes you pretty okay in my book."

She was right. He was only stressing himself out by worrying so much, and that didn't help anything. "Thanks, Deb."

"No problem. Now refill my coffee, would you? Most of mine ended up on the table somehow."

11

"How scary is it going to be?" Sage's hand slipped into Dex's as they waited in line.

"Well, I don't know for sure," he replied honestly. "Probably just a little bit scary, just enough to be fun."

She looked uncertain. "My friend Ella said her mom went to a haunted house."

Oh, boy. Here they went again with Ella. Dex had never realized just how much Sage would learn about life by sharing a classroom with other children who had big mouths. "Did she?"

"Uh huh. And she said it was *really* scary. It wasn't just the decorations, either. There were people with chainsaws who were trying to cut them in half! They were running after them and everything!"

"I see." There were haunted houses like that, but why would anyone come home and tell their young child about them? "Sometimes adults like to do things that feel really scary, and that's why they go to haunted houses like that. I know this one isn't that way, or I wouldn't have brought you."

"You're sure? No chainsaws?"

"No chainsaws. I promise. I'll be right here next to you the whole time, too." Dex had thought it would be fun to do a haunted house together, one that was geared toward children. That was before he knew Sage had been primed with stories of other horror attractions.

"Well, if there are any people with chainsaws, I'm not going to let them touch me," Sage affirmed.

Dex glanced around and then knelt in front of Sage. "You know, that makes me think of something I've been meaning to talk to you about."

"What?"

"I know you could get a little spooked in there, and sometimes we do things when we're scared or we don't have time to think," he began.

"I won't hit them," she promised.

He chuckled. "I know you won't. I just want to

remind you not to use any magic." Dex whispered the last few words so quietly that Sage had to lean close.

"I know, Daddy. You've told me that, and so has Tina." She gave him one of those looks she'd mastered from a very young age, the kind that said she really wasn't stupid and adults didn't need to talk to her like she was.

"Yes," he acknowledged, "and I know you've been very good about it. This is just a bit of a different situation, and I thought we should talk about it. Especially since you've been practicing so much."

As soon as she'd gotten home from school and had a snack, Sage had disappeared into her room. Dex went to quietly check on her an hour later, figuring she was probably exhausted from their late night at the Samhain party. Instead, he'd found her sitting on her bed, working diligently to rearrange her stuffed animals with her magic.

They reached the entryway to the haunted house, and Dex paid their fee. Then a woman dressed as a witch handed Sage a laser pointer. "This is your magic wand! You'll see many different creatures as you venture through our haunted house. If any of them are a little too scary, you only need to point your magic wand and they'll disappear!"

"Clever," Dex murmured. He took Sage's hand.

"Do you have any questions about how your magic wand works?" the witch asked kindly.

Sage grinned. "No. I know a lot about magic."

Dex let that go for the moment, but only because this was one of the very few times Sage would be able to say such things.

They wound their way through dark halls, swirling tunnels, and a room full of mirrors. As the witch had promised, several actors in full costume and makeup were posted throughout the building. The first few they passed were mild: a pirate, a princess, and a few more witches. They'd done a good job at gearing this toward children.

"He's not so scary," Sage giggled as they passed a werewolf who lurked in the corner of a darker room.

Even Dex was starting to relax. She was going to do just fine.

They passed Frankenstein, his huge frame lurking in a doorway off to the side. He groaned through his stitched mouth. Sage cuddled close to her father and whipped her magic wand, the red light of the laser pointer landing square on Frankenstein's chest. The monster turned and walked away, disappearing in an instant.

"That worked quite well," Dex noted, relieved that she'd used the laser and not her real magic.

Sage made a mummy and a ghost disappear next, but she let an alien stay next to his crashed spaceship with bright lights.

Another friendly witch now stood before them. "You've almost escaped! There are a lot of monsters behind this door. You must use your magic wand and get as many of them as you can. Do you think you can do that?"

Sage nodded bravely. "Yes!"

The witch let them into the next room. It was styled as a bridge that went over a firepit, with fake flames and glowing red lights beneath it. The wood had been distressed to look old and shaky, but it was sturdy under their feet. As promised, monsters appeared on either side as they crossed the bridge. Sage held tight to Dex's hand, but she flashed her laser pointer as they hurried across the bridge. Trolls, goblins, and ogres fell backward at the merest glimmer of her wand. They pushed through a big wooden door and into a brightly lit room where yet another witch greeted them.

"You did a great job! Come pick a prize from our treasure chest!" She took the laser pointer and guided them to a huge treasure chest that held an abundance of little plastic toys. "You may also have a snack and a drink to refresh yourself after such an adventure."

"That was so fun, Daddy!" Sage enthused as they each took a cupcake and a juice box over to a table. "I'm glad we got to do that."

"Me, too, kiddo. You did a great job. You were really brave."

"It wasn't that scary," she told him.

"Just enough to have fun?" he asked.

She thought about it for a moment. "Yeah. And there weren't any chainsaws."

"No, we didn't need any of those." Dex rolled his head from side to side, trying to work out some of the tension knots that were constantly in his shoulders. He worried so much about Sage, and her magical training had taken that up another notch. Right now, though, he was happy. He was close with his daughter, and this was a memory they'd share for a long time.

"Dex! How nice to run into you here!"

He looked up to see Vanessa, part of Debbie's trio, approaching their table and holding a little girl's hand. "Oh. Hello."

"This is my daughter, Lily. Could we sit with you two?"

"Of course." He gestured at the chairs on the other side. He didn't know Vanessa all that well, but he didn't want to be rude. "This is Sage."

"How was it, Sage?" Vanessa asked. "Did you have a good time?"

"It was great!"

Lily, however, didn't look quite as pleased with her experience. "I thought it was too scary."

"Aw, that's okay, honey," Vanessa said, gently smoothing her daughter's sandy brown hair. "It's supposed to be scary."

"But I don't like it," Lily replied, slumping in her seat.

"We'll just have to do something not as scary sometime soon." Vanessa looked back up at Dex. She put one elbow on the table and leaned toward him a little. "Wasn't that reunion amazing? I can't believe how many people came out! It was just like old times, but even better because there was no homework!"

Dex laughed politely. "Serena really put a lot of work into it." Not that he'd stuck around to experience it for very long. The class reunion had merely been a prelude to a much more important reunion with Tina.

"That's the thing," Vanessa said, her eyes

narrowing slightly. "Big events like that really do take a lot of effort to pull off. Did Debbie tell you that I'm working at the Academy now?"

"Are you? No, she hadn't mentioned that." Or if she had, Dex hadn't been paying attention.

"Yes! For a couple of years now. It's really great to be back on the old stomping grounds all the time and to see new batches of kids coming through."

Where was she going with this? Dex hoped beyond all hope that Vanessa wasn't trying to flirt with him. He didn't want to have to turn her down, nor did he want to deal with Sage's inevitable questions. "I'm sure."

"I'm right in the front office, so I get to know all of them. Especially the ones who are always trying to go home sick!" she laughed. "Each faculty member has to volunteer to help out with a few extracurricular activities a year. Did you know that?"

"I guess that explains why Coach Chapman directed the school play that time," Dex quipped.

"Yes! Exactly! That's what you get for not picking your activity right away!"

Now he was starting to understand. "And what are you in charge of?"

"The fall dance," she said, spreading out her hands to emphasize just how big and exciting it was supposed to be. "It's going to be great! Straw bales and corn stalks, scarecrows, pumpkins, you name it."

"I'm sure they'll enjoy that." He glanced at his watch, wishing he had some place he had to be. Right now would be the perfect moment to make his excuses, but Sage and Lily had scooted together and were playing with the little jointed plastic snakes they'd picked out of the treasure chest.

Vanessa tipped her head to the side and grimaced. "They will, but only if I can make it happen. You see, I've managed to wrangle enough staff members and parents to act as chaperones, but I don't have any help with decorating. It's *so* difficult to get people to volunteer these days. Is there any chance you could come and help?"

"Well, I don't know," Dex replied uncertainly. "I'm not a staff member, and Sage doesn't go to that school yet."

"Oh, that doesn't matter!" Vanessa quickly replied. She smiled widely, but desperation pinched her eyes. "It would just be for an hour or so to set up."

His schedule was already so busy. Dex worked a lot of hours, and he devoted almost all of his free time to Sage. He scratched the back of his neck. "I'm not much of a decorator."

"I want to do it!" Sage blurted out, suddenly no longer interested in the plastic snake. "I want to decorate for a party! I *really* like parties!"

"What a great idea!" Vanessa squealed. "You could help your daddy!"

There was no hope of getting out of it now. Dex looked at Sage. "This isn't a party you would get to go to. It's only for high school kids."

"Can I blow up some balloons?" she asked.

"Absolutely! It wouldn't be a party without balloons!" Vanessa replied.

Now, his plans were solidified, all without making a decision himself. "Then I guess we'll see you this weekend!"

"Yay!" Sage cheered. "Are you going to be there, Lily?"

"No, I've got gymnastics practice."

"You do gymnastics? I play soccer."

The girls were having such a good time that Dex hated to pull them apart, but it was starting to get late. He made sure he had Vanessa's contact info and then loaded Sage into the car. They talked on the way home, and even though he wasn't crazy about the idea of helping Vanessa, he was glad that he and Sage had this evening together.

"Oh, no!" Sage said when they got home and walked into the living room.

"What's the matter?"

"Look!" She held up her snake. The plastic pieces were jointed together so the snake could be held by the tail while it slithered in the air. One of those joints, however, had snapped.

"Hm. How did that happen?" Dex gently took it from her hands to get a closer look.

"I buckled him into the car with me to make sure he was safe!" she whined.

Dex fiddled with it for a moment, hoping to make a repair, but it just wasn't possible. "I think that might've been too much for him."

"No!" Sage snatched the two halves of the snake from his hands. She smashed them together, but of course, they didn't stay. "I didn't mean to!"

"It's all right, honey. I know it was an accident. Sometimes these things happen." He did his best to soothe her, but Dex could tell it would only go so far. Sage had finally hit the wall and was beyond tired. "Let's get you ready for bed, and we can talk about it in the morning."

Tears were running down her face now, and she didn't make any move toward her room. "But I liked that snake!"

"It was a very neat toy," he agreed. The thing was made of the cheapest plastic possible, and it was no wonder that it'd broken under only a slight amount of strain, but he'd enjoyed those sorts of toys when he was a kid, too. "It's a real bummer that it's broken."

"It's not fair!" she screamed, still holding the snake in her trembling hands.

"I understand," he said softly.

"No, you don't!" Her brow scrunched up, her mouth pursed tightly. The two halves of the plastic snake lifted up out of her palms.

"Sage," he warned, trying to keep his voice steady. "You need to stop that right now."

She didn't listen. With a flick of her wrist, she chucked the broken toy at the wall.

"Sage Marie Heywood!" Every last drop of patience was wrung out of him in a split second. "You do *not* use your magic to be destructive! You know better than that! Go to bed, right now!" He pointed down the hallway for emphasis.

She charged down the hall, screaming and crying, and her door slammed behind her.

His muscles twitched at the sound, and he wanted to yell at her all over again for slamming her door, but instead, he threw his hands into the air.

"What the hell," he said to himself. "I've tried her whole life to be patient, caring, and nurturing, just to get this in return."

Dex crossed the room to retrieve the broken snake. Ironically, it wasn't any more damaged than it'd been before Sage had thrown it.

The toy, however, wasn't the problem. Sage's control of her magic was.

12

Tina let herself in the back door of The Crystal Cauldron. She automatically reached for the light switch and shut off the alarm system, her fingers moving without any real thought required. Next, she turned on the lights for the front of the store and the point-of-sale computers and went to the main door.

There, she turned around and tried to observe the shop as though she were someone coming in for the first time. What worked and what didn't? Were any of the displays too close together? Did the layout make sense? If someone were looking for a specific item, would it feel natural to find it in a certain spot?

The back door thudded.

"Good morning!" Nia called from the back. She appeared in the doorway between the main store and the stockroom. "I brought doughnuts. Oh. You're doing your thing again."

"My thing," Tina repeated with a smile. "It's more than just 'a thing.' It's what keeps this place going. It's why people keep coming back."

"I'll have to check the online reviews, but I'm pretty sure no one ever wrote that they wanted to come back here just because the essential oils were in alphabetical order," Nia teased.

"No, because people don't really know what it is they want," Tina explained. "They just want their shopping experience to go smoothly, whatever that might mean. I do my best to make it happen. And actually, I had a woman compliment me on the store layout just last week."

"Really?" Nia got the window cleaner and a rag out from under the counter and went to the front of the store to polish any fingerprints that'd been left by wayward children.

"Yes. She told me how happy she was that the walkways were wide enough for a stroller to fit through. Apparently, another shop she'd visited was so cramped and narrow that she couldn't get more than a few feet inside the store." Tina had been thrilled at the compliment.

"I thought the aisles had to be at least wide

enough for a wheelchair to get through." Nia squinted and then rubbed the glass a little harder.

"They do, but it doesn't mean every shop owner actually does what they're supposed to. I imagine the store won't be open for long, but you know how it is this time of year. People are so eager to grab a few souvenirs that they'll go anywhere without a huge line." Tina looked up at the lights. "Do you think we should change the lighting temperature? Maybe something a little warmer."

Nia laughed. "No one can say you don't have a passion for what you do."

"You're right, and today I'm even more excited," Tina told her.

"Why?"

"It's shipment day! Obviously! I know you didn't walk past those two towering stacks of boxes that arrived last night and forget!" Tina hurried to the back, wanting to see how much she could accomplish before it was time to officially open.

Nia followed her. "Anything new this week?"

"I got some tarot decks from a different publisher that we weren't carrying before. I thought it'd be good to have a few more options. I think we have a couple of new incense sticks, too." Tina sliced through the packing tape on a box and opened it, rummaging through the contents to ensure everything on the packing list was accurate before distributing the items throughout the store.

"Oh, these are cute!" Nia opened a box full of wind chimes, all with various themes related to the shop. "Zodiac, celestial, black cats, lotus... These are so cute! It's too bad we didn't have these a little earlier. I think we might've sold out of them at the height of tourist season."

"I agree, and I ordered them in plenty of time, but the supplier had some computer issues and got behind. They'll still make good inventory. I just have to find a good place to put them." Tina opened the next box, which was smaller but also very heavy. It was full of carved crystal animals.

"Why don't we hang one of each up in the front windows?" Nia suggested. "That way, people can see them, and we can reuse that old candle display that we didn't know what to do with."

"Oh, Nia! That's a fantastic idea! I think I might have some hooks we can use to hang the display pieces from. Let me see." She rushed across the stockroom and rummaged around in a drawer.

"You're in an awfully good mood today," Nia noted.

"Of course, I am." Tina found the hooks she was

looking for. "It's shipment day, and that always makes me happy. Would you grab the stepladder?"

They returned to the front of the store. "I know it does, but I think it's more than that."

Tina checked the antique clock on the back wall and then flipped over the 'open' sign. She didn't mind if customers came in and saw them working on the display. "What do you think it is, oh wise one?"

Nia unfolded the stepladder and positioned it in the corner near the window. She shot her boss a grin. "A man."

"I already got a thorough interrogation from my sisters after Dex left the covenstead the other night," Tina told her as she climbed up the ladder and tested out one of the hooks.

"But you guys are so cute together!" Nia unboxed the windchime with the moon and stars and handed it up to her. "You, Dex, and Sage. You're like a sweet little family."

Tina smiled despite herself. She'd started thinking about the three of them like that, too. "It's too early for such things," she reminded both herself and Nia.

"Early in the morning or early in the relationship?" Nia quipped.

Tina shot her a look before hanging the windchime. She climbed back down the ladder, moving it a little further across the floor before she climbed up again. "It was really nice to have Dex and Sage at the covenstead. I think they fit in pretty well, and I admit it makes me think about the future. But you know by now what my history with him is like. I wanted this to work out for such a long time, and then I'd resigned myself to the fact that my mate was unattainable. It makes it hard to believe it could be true."

The next windchime that went up had seven stones, one in each of the colors of the rainbow, hanging from the center to represent the chakras. "Amanda might like this one," Tina noted.

"Speaking of Dex, isn't that him crossing the street?" Nia nodded toward the window.

As Tina stepped back down onto the floor, she spotted Dex charging toward the front of the store, his strides long and firm. His fists were curled at his sides, and his mouth was a short, hard line. "Yeah, but he doesn't look too pleased."

"I've got this." Nia held her hand out for the hooks.

"No rush." She turned to the door just as Dex walked in. "Hey!"

"I need to talk to you."

She took half a step back. His aura flamed out from him in dark red with flashes of black. He was angry, but there was also some sort of emotional struggle going on inside him. "We can go back here."

Tina brought him through a side door and into a private room separated from the stock area. This space was small, but it made her think of an old library with its numerous shelves and cabinets that lined the walls. She gestured toward a chair at the long table in the center of the room. "Have a seat."

"I don't know if I can." He glanced around. "What is this room?"

"It's where I keep all the serious stuff," she explained. Even if he wasn't going to sit, she did. "Grimoires, records, supplies that are rare or potent. Anything out front would be harmless for someone who's just a beginner. Not so much in here."

"Mm," he grunted as he gripped the back of the chair so hard, his knuckles turned white. "Magic is just what I came here to talk to you about."

"Dex, just tell me what's wrong," she encouraged gently.

He pulled in a deep breath. "Sage got angry last night over a broken toy. She used her magic to throw it against the wall."

Tina clucked her tongue. "I see."

"I don't think you do," he countered. "She's only been getting lessons for about a week, and already, she's used her magic in anger. I can't have this, Tina."

"I get it," she replied, folding her hands on the table. "I'll have a talk with her."

"You *don't* get it. Sage won't be coming to you for lessons anymore," he announced. His jaw was set, and his eyes sparked with anger.

Tina felt her own anger rising inside her. "I don't think that's a very good idea."

"I didn't ask you what you think. I'm telling you that this is all wrong. If Sage is already this destructive, then she's better off not learning anything else. If it's a junky, plastic toy today, what's it going to be tomorrow?"

"Possibly nothing. Like I told you before, this is all about emotional control and awareness. It's also knowledge and experimentation. Sage will understand that what she did last night was wrong. Maybe she needed to make that mistake in order to learn from it, and then she'll have that much more experience to build on as she continues her journey." She searched for all the right words, wanting to really make him understand how important it was that Sage kept learning.

"She can make a mistake when she's learning her

multiplication tables or when she starts learning how to cook. And what are the repercussions? A few missed points? Some burned brownies? Big deal. But we're talking about something far more serious, Tina."

"I'm well aware of that." The anger was vibrating in her bones now. "That's precisely why she needs to get a hold of it now."

"What makes you think you're qualified to be the one who teaches her?" he snapped.

"May I remind you that you felt I was perfectly qualified when this whole thing started?" she whipped back. "You asked me to."

"I guess I was wrong." He slapped his palm on the back of the chair. "I guess I was wrong about a lot of things."

"So, Sage isn't the only one who makes mistakes sometimes," Tina pointed out.

"I'm her father, all right? I'm the one who calls the shots. Not you or anyone else."

"Then I guess you can go call the shots somewhere else." She rose from her seat, but she kept her hands on the table for a moment so he couldn't see how unsteady they were. Her gaze, at least, was focused like a laser on him. "I'm not going to listen to any more of this. You know where to find me when you're ready to listen and look for a solution. Bye, Dex."

He turned and left without even saying goodbye.

Tina stood there for a long moment, feeling her wolf thrash inside her. It knew, just as she did, that this wasn't simply Dex going home for the night or having to get to work. This parting went far deeper than that. She didn't know if she'd ever see him again.

Slowly, she sank back down into the chair and covered her face with both of her hands. She pressed her cool fingertips against her heated skin. This wasn't how any of this was supposed to happen.

"Hey," Nia said quietly from the doorway. "Are you okay?"

Tina slid her hands off her face.

"I saw him blow out of here like a hurricane," Nia explained. "Figured I'd check on you."

It took her a moment to answer. She pulled in a breath and let it out through her nose. "Yeah. I'm fine. Or at least, I'm good enough."

"Do you need anything? Hot tea? Some of those doughnuts I brought?" Nia offered.

Stuffing her face with sweet, fried dough sounded like a great solution to her problem, but it was only a temporary one that would make her feel like shit later. "No, thank you. All I really need to do is get back to work and on with my life."

"You sure? I can handle the rest of the windchime display."

Tina stood and walked out of the room, closing the door behind her. "I know you can, but I'm better off if I'm busy right now. If Dex wants to be mad, then he can just go be mad. He can even believe I'm the problem if he wants to. I've got things to do, no matter how he feels."

"I'm going to go turn on some music," Nia said decisively, heading into the back. A few moments later, some loud rock came over the speakers.

"This isn't the meditation music I usually play in here," Tina said when she returned.

"I know," Nia replied brightly. "I just thought we could use it. You know, get a little energy in here while we work."

Her wolf whined and paced inside her. Tina's heart was split, and her mind was distracted. This was just what she needed. Music and work wouldn't fix her problems, but at least they'd make her feel better for a short time.

"All right, then. Let's get to it."

13

DEX BURST INTO THE HEYWOOD PACKHOUSE. HE turned down the hallway to check his father's den, but it was empty. Next, he hurried upstairs to his mother's reading and sewing room. It, too, was empty. Most of the pack that lived there were off at work, apparently, and the place felt eerily quiet. It bothered the hell out of him, especially because he didn't feel quiet at all.

The front door slammed, and he charged down the stairs to see who it was. Debbie was just coming in, her cell phone braced between her cheek and her shoulder. "No, they said they had to move the talent show. I know a lot of people were bummed, but it'll work out well for us."

She glanced up as Dex came rattling down the

stairs. Her brows furrowed for a second. "Hey, honey. Can I call you back? Yeah. Okay, that sounds good. Love you." She pulled the phone away from her cheek and hung up.

"How's Tom?"

Debbie gave him an appraising look. "I think the real question is how are *you*. The pissiness is just rolling off of you in waves right now."

"That bad, huh?" He sat on the bottom step and then got back up again, too aggravated to sit still at the moment.

She snickered. "Yeah, I'd say. What's going on?"

Dex had automatically come to the packhouse after he'd left The Crystal Cauldron. He needed a place that felt calmer and steadier, a place where he could just let it all out. It was harder than he thought, though. "I don't know where to start. My feelings around all of this are pretty complicated."

"Then let's go for a run," she suggested. "I was just popping by to drop off some kitchen stuff I'd borrowed from mom, but I've got a little free time."

He shook his head, suddenly feeling guilty at the idea of taking up her time, but Dex knew he needed to get all of this off his chest. If he could do that with anyone, it would be his twin. "All right."

They went through the house and out the back

door. The packhouse had an expansive backyard, surrounded by lush trees. It was the perfect place for young pups to practice their shifting, wrestle and play with each other, and learn how to tap into their lupine selves. When they were in their human form, there was also a large jungle gym for them to play on. It was a paradise for a child.

Dex wished he could have the simple life of a child, of not having to worry about much more than what shirt he'd wear to school or what kind of jelly to have on his peanut butter sandwich.

He stepped off the deck and brought his wolf forward. It came quickly, both from practice and from need. It'd been boiling inside of him ever since he'd left The Crystal Cauldron. His bones cracked swiftly into place, and his furry ears shot forward. As soon as his paws touched the grass, he took off.

I'd say you really needed this, Debbie said, a short way behind him, but holding steady.

I don't know how humans get through the hard parts of life when they can't do something like this. There was no better way to work through his emotions, to release anger and frustration, and then dig deep into the real problem. Even when life was perfect, there was something invigorating about feeling the wind ruffle through his fur and pushing off against the bare earth.

Debbie was starting to catch up to him now as they hit a curve in the path. *They punch pillows or yell at their coworkers. Or drink.*

I could drink all I want, and it won't make this go away. He slowed down a little. A recent storm had left a large branch over the path, and he squeezed underneath it.

Tell me. She cursed as a smaller twig on the branch caught her fur.

This was why he went to Debbie. When she said, 'Tell me,' it wasn't a command. It was an invitation, but one that she expected him to accept. It was just another part of their connection, and he cherished it.

Now, he was trotting, moving quickly enough to still let some of his energy out, but making it easier to talk. *Sage misused her magic last night.*

Debbie moved slightly to the side in surprise. *Did she hurt anyone?*

No, nothing like that. He explained how Sage had thrown her toy against the wall in frustration. *I just couldn't believe she'd used her magic like that! It's not like this isn't something we've discussed.*

She's a kid, Debbie reasoned. *They do all sorts of*

things that don't make sense. I've been through the gamut with my two. It doesn't always matter how much you've talked about something, either. It needs to be repeated a million times, and they probably still won't get it.

You're not making me feel any better. If she can't listen and do the right thing, she's not going to be allowed to use her magic at all. He sent the words to her with all the firmness he could. Someone had to take him seriously.

You don't really mean that, do you? she asked after a silent moment.

Absolutely. If she were old enough to have a driver's license and got a speeding ticket, I wouldn't let her drive. Magic is something she has to learn to handle responsibly. He noted a few other limbs that were down and would need to be taken care of.

They looped around the path, careful not to get too close to the property line and risk being seen. Debbie looked up, a little more cautious there where the trees were thinner. *Dex, I can't claim to understand what you're going through completely. I know having magic makes things complicated. But driving a car is a privilege, and magic is something she was born with.*

That doesn't mean she can wait to control herself until she's old enough, he snapped.

Maybe if she learned—

Then she'd end up just like me, Dex told her, finally getting out the point he'd been beating himself against this whole time. *A plastic snake is one thing, but what if that'd been another kid who took her toy? No. I won't have it, and that's why she's not seeing Tina anymore, either.*

Though Debbie didn't immediately say anything about that, Dex could feel the tension through their psychic connection.

What about you? she finally asked. *Are you seeing Tina anymore?*

I highly doubt it. He brooded on that last conversation with Tina. No, not conversation. Argument. She'd been trying to keep her calm, but she couldn't control the fury that flew from her eyes.

They were heading back toward the house now, although they could continue to make loops on the path for as long as they wanted to. Debbie took the first turn that would keep them going instead of bringing them to the yard. *You're torturing yourself.*

No, I'm not.

You are, and you're dragging Sage into it. Don't you dare lay into me for being honest, either, she shot just as Dex was getting ready to do exactly that. *You know me, and you wouldn't come to me for anything but the honest truth.*

Yes, but I can't just let her lessons continue if they're not good for her. And I can't keep seeing Tina if she doesn't understand what's really going on with Sage. We're a package deal. We can't be split up.

Debbie angled to the side, taking a narrower path so they could avoid the downed branch this time around. *I think Tina is the last person who'd try to separate you. From everything you've said, she genuinely cares about Sage.*

I thought so, too, but not after the conversation I just had with her. This was their 'secret path' as kids, one that deer had made. It twisted and turned before rejoining with one of the larger trails.

Ah, so that's why you were still so angry when you got here. Sage threw her toy last night, but the showdown with Tina happened today. She'd pushed ahead of him, keeping her pace slow and steady, forcing him to do the same.

That only made him feel like running again. *I wouldn't call it a showdown.*

An argument, then? It couldn't have been a calm and reasonable conversation, or your head wouldn't be boiling over. When you first shifted, I thought my own head was going to explode just from what'd made it over here to me.

Pfft. He took a long stride so his front paw came down on her back one, tripping her.

Shit! You're such a brat. I mean it, though. I haven't seen you that mad in a long time, Debbie told him.

They emerged onto a wider trail again, this time on a loop that led near a small creek. *She refused to listen to reason.*

And did you come in there like a steam engine, the same way you came here? Debbie challenged.

His vision had been so red with anger and frustration that Dex could hardly even remember driving to The Crystal Cauldron. He only knew that he had to talk to Tina about this, and he couldn't wait another second. *Probably, but I had a right to be.*

She left the path and descended to the creek, letting her paws sink into the shallow mud on its bank. Debbie's sharp wolf eyes bored into his. *If she had thrown the toy with her hands, would you have reacted the same way and burned down your connection with Tina?*

He lifted his chin defiantly. *If I thought Tina was the reason she threw it, then I might.*

Kids make mistakes, Dex. Debbie stuck a paw in the water experimentally, shaking it out when the water was too cold.

Just to show her up, Dex trotted across the shallow creek. It was cold as hell, a sign of the coming winter, but he didn't show his discomfort.

Sure, but this wasn't just a normal fit. She used magic to make it happen. I don't think you can compare the two situations.

Debbie walked a little way along the creek, looking for a narrow spot. *Do you remember when she first started to play soccer?*

He didn't want to answer that. Debbie would lead him down some logical path where she would prove him wrong. *Of course.*

She was really excited. She liked the uniform and the ball. You had to bring her over so I could help you guys figure out how to do her hair for games. She started watching professional women's games on TV and talking about how strong those women were. Sage was going to work hard and be just like them. Debbie flexed her haunches and hopped across the creek, only getting one of her back paws wet. She shook it out and then hurried up the other side of the bank.

I remember. How could he forget? Soccer had been Sage's entire life for a few months. She still played, but the obsession had eventually slowed down.

They walked side by side now, the morning sun casting their shadows onto the undergrowth. *Then a few weeks into her first season, she made her first goal. Unfortunately, it was in the wrong net.*

He'd lived her heartache for her, both when he'd realized what'd happened and when Sage had gotten the news from her coach. *She was absolutely devastated.*

And what did you tell her? You didn't make her quit. You explained that this was just a good lesson to learn so she knew what to do next time. Unless I missed something, I don't believe she's ever kicked the ball into the wrong goal again.

Dex let out an inward sigh. *I get it, Deb. I know what you're saying. But this is* magic *we're talking about. Doing the wrong thing could have real consequences.*

So could completely leaving it behind, she pointed out sharply. *And what about you and Tina?*

He turned his head, pretending to watch a squirrel. *That doesn't matter.*

Yes, it does! This could be your last chance to be with your true mate. You had a great relationship with Marie. She was a sweet person, and I don't regret getting to know her. But something was always lacking, something sad around the edges of that relationship because you knew you weren't fated. You've always wanted that.

Dex had the feeling she'd be poking him in the chest with her finger if they were in their human forms. *Sage's wellbeing is more important than any of my selfish needs.*

Damn it! Debbie leaned over and nipped his ear. *You've never been selfish, Dex, and there's absolutely nothing selfish about wanting something for yourself. I've already told you this, but I'll say it a thousand times if I have to.*

Debbie—

And maybe, just maybe, you're actually being selfish right now by cutting Tina out of your life. She stopped after that, letting it sink in.

They walked back to the packhouse in silence. As they reached the deck, they returned to their human forms. Being on two legs felt heavy and cumbersome, but Dex knew that was only because of his dark mood. He understood what Debbie was saying, and in some circumstances, he was probably right. This was magic, though. It changed everything.

She checked the time as they got inside. "I've got to go, Dex."

"Thank you for spending time with me, even if you think I'm an ass," he replied.

Debbie gave him a firm look. "I do, but I also love you. I wouldn't get so riled up if I didn't care. I know that's essentially your problem, too, but you've got to relax and let go a little. You've got to think about what's going to be best for you in the long run. Sage is still young, but she won't always be right there at your side."

"No," he acknowledged, though the thought was a knife through his heart, "but I'm the only person she has right now."

Debbie shook her head. "No. You're not. You've been working so hard to compensate for being a single parent, but maybe you don't need to do that. At least think about it, Dex. I'll see you later." She headed out to her car.

He couldn't help but mull it over as the day went on. Debbie's words echoed in his brain as though she were still there next to him. She made it sound so simple, like he could just follow his heart and everything would be fine. Life had taught him the opposite.

Later that evening, after he'd picked Sage up from school and they'd had dinner, he tucked her in for the night.

"Daddy?"

"Yes, honey?" He sat on the edge of her bed, glad that they'd managed to have a good afternoon together. She'd told him all about the projects she was working on in school, who was doing what on the playground, and how gross the cafeteria food could be.

Sage's eyes were especially big when she looked up at him. "I'm sorry I threw my toy yesterday."

His heart melted, and the tension flooded out of his muscles. "I'm glad to hear that, and I'm sorry I got angry with you."

"That's okay. I know what I did was bad, and I won't do it again," she promised solemnly.

"Good."

"When do I get to see Tina next? I wanted to ask her some questions." She fiddled with her doll's hair.

He hated to have this conversation right after they'd made up, but it needed to happen. "You actually won't be seeing her again. I've thought about it a lot after last night, and I've decided that your magical training needs to wait until you're older."

She shot upright in bed. "But I said I was sorry!"

"I know, and I appreciate that. It's important to make up for the things we've done. I also know it's hard for you to understand why all of this has to stop when you've been having fun, but it's not really about fun. Magic can be dangerous, and it needs to wait until you're older."

"That's not fair!" She fell back on her pillow with

a thump and rolled over, her doll tucked firmly under her arm.

"We can talk about this," Dex said gently as he laid his hand on her arm. Despite what Tina or Debbie said, he really did know it would be difficult for Sage. That didn't mean it wasn't right.

Sage squirmed out from under his arm. "No. I don't want to talk to you. I like Tina, I like my lessons, and I like my magic."

He understood what was implied there. Right now, Sage didn't like him. He wasn't going to convince her otherwise. The best thing he could do was to give her time to cool off. "Goodnight, honey."

He went out into the living room and turned on the TV, but it couldn't hold his attention for more than a few seconds. Everyone was angry with him, and it made him feel like he'd lost everything.

14

Tina flipped over the sign and locked the door. She'd worked hard, putting every ounce of her energy into her store and her customers, and now she was paying for it. Her muscles were sore. Her head ached. She wasn't sure she had the energy even to go home and take a shower.

"Any weekend plans?" she asked Nia.

"Gavin and I are going to a concert." Nia was behind the counter, balancing the cash register and putting the deposit together.

"One of his concerts, or someone else's?"

"A friend of his. Gavin played me a sample of their music, and they sound pretty good. They think they're going to get signed soon, and Gavin is hoping they can put in a good word for him." Nia smiled as she zipped up the deposit bag. "I think he actually has a chance of making it."

"What's the name of his band again?" Tina could never remember, but that was partly because it'd changed several times.

"Echoes of Tomorrow," Nia replied. "I think it'd look pretty good on an album cover. Anyway, what about you? Doing anything this weekend?"

Tina frowned. "Probably not."

"Oh, right. Sorry."

"No, it's fine." Tina had stayed busy enough that even she had managed to forget a few times, though those moments of peace probably only lasted a few seconds each. "I'll have the store open tomorrow, and Colette will be here."

"Want me to take this?" Nia held up the deposit bag.

"No, I will." Tina put it in her bag while Nia shut down the computer. They turned off the lights, set the alarm, and locked the back door behind them.

As Tina got in her car and waved to Nia, she felt the night closing in on her. For years, it'd never been an issue to go home to an empty apartment. It was fine, really, because it meant she could do whatever she wanted. She had true freedom, and she enjoyed it.

Tonight, though, as she parked her car and walked inside, the warm and cozy space she'd curated felt cold and lonely.

"I can stay here and feel sorry for myself, or I can do something about it," she said as she took out her phone and fired off a text message.

Tina stopped at the liquor store on her way to the covenstead and arrived with a few new bottles of wine. "I've never tried any of these," she said as she, Amanda, and Chelsea got set up on the back porch. The evening was cool, but the sun had been shining in through the screens all day. It was the perfect mix for a night outside.

Amanda lit a few candles on the patio table for ambient lighting. "Hey, I'm always up for trying something new! I was glad when you texted, because I wasn't sure what to do tonight."

Chelsea nodded in agreement. She was setting down a hefty charcuterie board that looked incredible. "Beck and Corbin already had plans for a daddy-son night, so this was perfect. Is anyone else joining us?"

"I think it's just us three." Tina opened one of the bottles of wine and filled their glasses. "There's a lot of power in that number, though."

"One of my favorites," Amanda agreed. She took

a small sip of the wine and raised her brows. "That's nice."

Chelsea tried it next and nodded her approval. "Reds have never been my favorite, but that's pretty smooth."

Tina raised her glass to her lips, truly glad that she hadn't spent the whole evening just wallowing around in her place, feeling sorry for herself. She took a long sip of wine, trusting her sister and cousin. It was just as good as they promised, and she relaxed into her chair. "How was your day, Amanda? I know you've been pretty packed at work."

"I have, and that's part of the reason I was so eager to take you up on this invitation. I'm supposed to be adjusting my clients' energies, helping their bodies and their spirits align, but it's rough when they're all coming in back-to-back and I barely have time to pee."

"Sounds to me like you need to give yourself a break," Chelsea advised. "If your practice is doing that well, maybe it's time to bring on someone new."

"I thought about it." Amanda held her glass by the stem and swirled it slowly. "I'd have to be really careful, though. If I bring the wrong person in, it could be disastrous."

"Or wonderful," Tina pointed out. "Do you

remember when I first opened the shop? I didn't trust anyone else to help me run the place. The next thing I knew, I had to close down every time I had an emergency or got sick. That's not great for business."

Amanda narrowed one of her wide brown eyes as she pointed a finger at Tina. "You've had some real flakes in there."

"A few," Tina admitted, "but a lot of them have been good. I've had some pretty steady employees, and of course, Nia and Collette have been amazing. Nia, especially, is getting to the point that she's coming up with new ideas and displays."

"You could just put the word out with people you know," Chelsea suggested. "That might be better than just a general help wanted ad."

"Yeah, I could look around." Amanda helped herself to a cheese cube. "What about you, Chels? You've probably been just as busy as the rest of us."

"Oh, sure. I've had several requests for birth charts over the past month, both in person and online, but so far, I've been able to manage. I do need to make some upgrades to my website, though."

After they'd shot a few ideas about that back and forth, Tina smiled. "You know what's funny? I said we should get together to relax, but all we talk about is work!"

"You're right." Chelsea turned in her seat and looked straight into Tina's face. "So, why don't we tackle the elephant in the room. Tell us what happened between you and Dex."

Tina stuffed a couple of cheese cubes in her mouth. "Who said anything happened?"

"Your face," Amanda supplied. "Your aura."

"The way you're holding your wine glass like you might break it," Chelsea added. "Or perhaps it's those dark circles under your eyes that say you've worked yourself even harder than usual."

"Hey!" Tina touched her face self-consciously, but she knew Chelsea was right. She could feel how tired her eyes were every time she blinked.

"That's true." Amanda gave Tina an analytical look. "You look like you did just after you graduated high school."

"I'd love that to be a compliment, but I have a feeling it's not," Tina retorted. "Also, I don't know what you're talking about."

Chelsea plucked a slice of salami from the tray. "You and Dex had spent four years on the will-they-won't-they rollercoaster, but there was still a chance it'd work out as long as you were still in school. Once graduation came, you knew that was the end."

"And that's when you started throwing yourself even harder into studying and work." Amanda picked up the story for her. "Not that you weren't always a hard worker, but that's when you started doing it to the point of exhaustion."

"Which looks like it happened today." Chelsea polished off the last sip of wine. "Let's try the second bottle, and you could tell us."

Tina opened the Moscato, laughing uncertainly. "I knew I needed some time with you guys, but I thought I could just relax and talk about this when I was ready."

"Oh, hell no." Amanda held out her glass. "Pour the wine and spill the tea. We'll just drag it out of you if you don't."

"Clearly." She sat back down and told them about Dex coming to the shop that morning. "I get that Sage losing a little control was upsetting for him, but he just went completely off the rails."

"Hm." Chelsea chewed a cracker thoughtfully. "Sounds to me like he's scared."

"Really?"

"Oh, sure. Being a parent is absolutely terrifying. You're just guessing all the time. You have to make tons of choices, and for some, you won't know if they were the right ones for years down the road. I think about it with Corbin, although I try not to get too caught up in it." She gave Tina a wistful smile. "It's hard when you love them so much."

"But I love Sage, too." Tina's heart ached as she thought of that sweet little girl. "I know she isn't mine. I don't have the right to say what happens in her life. I just hate the idea of not getting to spend time with her anymore."

Amanda flicked her dark hair behind her so that it hung over the back of the chair. "And what about Dex? Is he part of that fantasy picture, too?"

Tina couldn't lie. Not to them. Even if she tried, they'd figure her out as they'd already proven. "Yeah. Recently, anyway. For a long time, I'd let myself believe that I'd never get to be with him. Then he just waltzed right into my life again. We'd had all that stupid social status crap that'd kept us apart when we were younger, but we're old enough now that it's gone. I thought that meant we could finally make it work."

Chelsea reached over and rubbed her arm. "Maybe you still can. An argument doesn't have to be the end of things."

"It was a pretty big argument." Tina didn't think

she'd ever seen that look on Dex's face before. Chelsea was probably right, and that was all because he was scared for his child's future. That was understandable, but it'd just been so hard. "The way he lashed out at me has me second-guessing the whole thing."

"Didn't he have a magical fight with some kid back in the day?" Amanda asked.

"Oh, yeah. That's been brought up a few times since I started teaching Sage." She sighed and sipped the Moscato, which was far lighter and brighter than she felt inside. "I wish I could get him to understand that he was just a kid, and that he can't really hold himself responsible for that anymore."

"His own experiences are making him overprotective," Chelsea concluded. "That sucks, and I hate that he's beating himself up over something he did so long ago, but you can't really change who a person is or how they think. You either have to decide that you're good with how things are, or that you're not going to put up with it."

Tina thought about this as she rolled her glass stem between her fingers. "Did you second-guess yourself on getting back together with Beck? When you weren't sure if the Beck you knew was still around?" A sorcerer had put a powerful mindwipe spell on Beck. It was enough to make him forget who he was, and it'd taken a lot of time, love, and magic to get him back.

"Shit, yes," she told Tina. "You still feel that pull inside you, that connection that has always been there, but that beast inside you doesn't understand logic. It doesn't know how complicated a relationship could be. It only knows what it wants and damn the consequences."

Tina let out a long sigh, something she'd been doing all day and was likely to continue doing for a while yet. "I just don't know what to do. My mind keeps wrestling with it, like this is a problem I have to find a solution for."

Amanda was flicking her thumb and pointer finger toward the candles, sending miniature energy waves into the flames and making them dance. She stopped and looked up at her cousin. "I know this doesn't really help, but you have to do what's right for you, for your heart and your life. That might mean being with Dex, and it might not. You know we're here for you all the way, but we can't decide for you."

"Life would be a whole lot easier if you could," Tina grumbled.

"I don't know. You didn't even like it when I used to give you advice on what to wear," Chelsea teased. "You hated it when I told you what to do."

"Yes," Tina said with a little laugh. "I guess I still do."

"Is there any direction you're leaning?" Amanda asked, playing with the candle flames again.

There was just enough wine in her system to make her slow down, to allow her to really pull back and see the big picture a little more objectively. She had a thing for Dex, and it honestly came from both sides of her. It'd be wonderful if they could make it work out.

Right now, though, she wanted something even more than to have her mate at her side. "I want to help Sage," she said. "I don't know exactly how, and I need to give myself the space and time to think about it, but that's the one thing I know for sure I have to do. She's lost her mother, and she doesn't have anyone to guide her with her magic. That's not a situation any young witch should be put in."

"That sounds like a solution to me," Chelsea said. She lifted her glass. "To solutions, even if they're vague and temporary, but as long as they make us feel better!"

Tina and Amanda laughed as they clinked their glasses against hers. "To solutions!"

"Thanks, you guys. I'll keep you posted. I'm glad I've got you. I might not know what the hell I was doing otherwise."

"Eh, I'd say most of us don't," Chelsea said. "We just have to wing it the best we can."

Tina laughed and talked well into the night with her sister and cousin, but still felt uncertain. She didn't have any real plan as to how to help Sage, and Dex might not even let her. Her stomach clenched. Tears threatened every time she thought of Dex, and worry rippled under her skin when she thought about Sage. But at least it was just a little better.

15

"This is going to be really fun, Daddy!" Sage said from the backseat.

"Yes, it is." Dex still wasn't thrilled that he'd been roped into decorating for the fall dance at the Academy, but he might as well make the best of it.

"Wait, don't we need to bring the decorations?"

"No, honey. Vanessa's bringing all those."

"Oh, the lady we met at the haunted house?"

Dex turned off the main road. He could see a few people out on the football field, throwing balls around. "Yep."

"She seemed nice. Did she go to school with you?"

Sage was chock full of questions that afternoon, but he wasn't about to make that stop. It was far better than the way she'd been when he'd first woken her up with pancakes and scrambled eggs. Sage had eaten them begrudgingly, only deigning to speak to her father when she needed him to pass the butter.

What had followed was a long and exhausting discussion about magic. Sage had managed to convince him to at least let her continue to do the magic she knew. Dex had convinced her that she still had plenty to learn and that she'd have to heed his advice.

He worried that he'd caved, but some of Tina and Debbie's arguments had haunted him through the night. Telling Sage not to do any magic was akin to telling her not to read or color or laugh. It was a natural part of her, and he had to settle for things slowing down, even if he couldn't get them to stop completely.

At least the two of them were back on good terms. Dex just wondered how long it'd be before Sage started negotiating for more. Kids would always push the envelope.

"Here we are." He secured a spot right next to the school, as it was a late Saturday afternoon and very few others were present.

Sage got out of the car and tipped her head all

the way back as she took in the height of the building. "This is where you went to school?"

"Sure is."

"But it's so old!" she exclaimed.

Dex had to laugh a little at that. "This building had already been standing for well over a hundred years by the time I went to school here, so it's always been old." He'd never appreciated that when he was younger, thinking that the shiny new buildings he saw elsewhere had to be far better. Granted, their heating was probably a lot more even, and they might not have creaky wooden floors, but Dex knew now that a place like this had a lot more character.

He brought her into the entryway. It'd felt strange to see it all again when he'd come there for the reunion, but now he was taking it in through the eyes of someone completely new to it. "There's the trophy case. It shows all the various awards that the school has won over the years. And if you look right up there on the wall, there's a class photo for every single class of students who graduated from here."

Sage peered at a photo of the graduating class of '52. "Which one are you?"

"That's around the time your great-grandpa graduated!" He laughed, bringing her further down the hall and pointing at his own class. "I'm in this one. See if you can find me."

"Umm..." Sage leaned close, tapping her finger on her lips. "That one!"

"Are you sure?" Dex asked. "Why do you think that one is me?"

"Because you're making that face when you're trying not to laugh," she replied wisely.

"So I am. If I remember right, some of the other guys were clowning around. Let's get in the gym and see what Vanessa needs." He headed for the door.

"Wait!" She was still staring at the photo.

"What is it?" Dex patiently walked backward a couple of steps.

Sage pointed, keeping her finger hovering just above the glass. "That's Tina!"

"Yes." He didn't have to push his face up to the frame to know what she looked like. Dex had seen that photo many times. He'd flipped through his yearbook every now and then for several years after graduating, wondering what could've been between them. It was usually when he was feeling most alone, or when yet another one of his friends had found their true mate and paired off.

"She's really pretty," Sage said, a wistful note in her voice.

Tina was sitting in the front row of the bleachers. Her hair was a bit longer back then, draping down in front of her and hiding some of her natural curves. She had cat-eye glasses that were popular at the time, although they truly looked good on her. The camera had caught her with just a hint of a smile, as though she knew something that no one else did.

"Yes, she was," Dex agreed.

"She still is," Sage countered.

"Vanessa is waiting for us." He gestured toward the gym doors, glad when Sage left the photo and followed him. Dex didn't want to think about Tina. He'd known for a very long time that he was never going to have her. Recent events had only proven him right.

They walked into the gym to find Vanessa standing amidst a giant pile of boxes and bags. She was dressed in a hot pink halter top and black leggings, and her dark hair was pulled back into two short pigtails.

"Ah, there you are!" she exclaimed when they walked in. "I was just starting to get worried."

"Did I have the time wrong?" Dex glanced at his watch. They were five minutes early as far as he knew.

"No, it's not that." Vanessa's brow wrinkled as she

bit her lip. "It's that no one else has shown up! I hoped we'd have a nice little group of people here, so we could get it all done quickly, but I guess everyone either forgot or decided they had something better to do."

"That's not very nice," Sage asserted.

Vanessa gave her a smile. "You're right, but we have to make the best of it!"

"What can we do?" Dex asked.

"Anything you want. I've got to run to the store and pick up a few more things. I completely forgot to get tea lights. Another mom was supposed to pick up a bunch of pumpkins for the photo booth, but since she's not here, I've got to get those, as well." Vanessa was always bright and perky, but the stress of this party was beginning to crack her façade.

"I don't know much about decorating, but we'll do our best," Dex promised.

"I can make it really pretty!" Sage exclaimed.

"Sounds to me like it's in good hands, then!" Vanessa chirped. To Dex, she said, "And really, I'm not picky. I just want to make sure the kids have a good party."

"You've got it."

Vanessa dashed off, leaving the two of them alone.

Dex looked around. The gym was a massive space for two people to decorate, especially when one of them was a child. It'd been all done up for the reunion, but that had been taken down, and it was back to just being a gym. He went to the pile of items that Vanessa had already brought and began looking through them to take inventory. "Let's see. We've got crepe paper, baskets, balloons—"

"I want to do the balloons!" Sage hopped up and down and clapped her hands.

"Do you know how to blow them up?" Dex pulled out a bag, opened it, and handed her one.

Sage looked at it for a second. She put her lips up to the end and blew, but could only get it into a flattened sphere.

"You've got to stretch it out a little." Dex went back and forth with Sage a few times, showing her how to stretch the balloon, how to get it big enough without popping it, and then how to tie it off.

"I did it!" She held the balloon out so he could admire the knot she managed to make.

"You sure did. Now, we have to decide where to put them. We can't just tape them to the bleachers. That won't be very exciting. I've got to see if there's a ladder around here somewhere." He'd found several rolls of tape that Vanessa had left for them, but he was starting to realize just how much the lack of directions was going to slow them down.

"Wait, Daddy." Sage held the orange balloon she'd just blown up at arm's length. It slowly lifted from her hands, rising toward the ceiling even though it was filled with regular air instead of helium. It glided gently up until it was high on the wall, just under the row of windows.

His stomach curled in on itself at the idea of her using magic there. Dex had to remind himself that even though at times this was a busy place, they were the only ones there. He'd also promised Sage that he'd do his best to guide her, and getting angry or anxious wasn't going to work. "You did a good job. Now, how are we going to make it stay there?"

"Oh, I know!" Sage dropped her hands, letting the orange balloon drift back down. She caught it before it hit the floor and put a piece of tape on the end. Then she sent it skywards again. It took her a bit of concentration to push it hard enough into place for the tape to stick, but she managed.

"You're pretty clever," Dex told her, genuinely meaning it. Sage was using her magic, but she was also using her mind. She was a brilliant girl. Who was he to stop her growth?

The doubt in him also wanted to know who he

was to think he had any right to teach her. He'd lost control. He'd nearly killed someone. Plenty of people had told him to stop berating himself over that incident, but that was easy for them to say.

Of course, if he wasn't the one to guide her, then who would? It couldn't be Tina. He'd already drawn a hard line against that, both with Tina and with Sage. There was no going back.

Sage's giggling pulled him out of his dark and muddled thoughts.

"This is fun!" She'd just sent a black balloon skyward. Clusters of balloons in twos and threes were now gathered all along the top of the wall.

"I think you've got a knack for decorating. Should we put some streamers up there with them?" Dex showed her the roll of crepe paper.

"How do we do that?" Her eyes were alight with excitement.

He peeled open the end of the roll and put a piece of tape on it before handing it to her. "We can put some up that goes from one bunch of balloons to the next."

She grinned at him as she took the end and sent it flying up to its proper spot. "You do the other end, Daddy!"

Heat flushed his cheeks, and fear stormed his

body. His stomach was now a raging sea. But Dex had made a promise. Sage was the most important thing in the world to him. He tore off the end of the streamer and attached a piece of tape to it.

The only magic he'd practiced in years had been the healing light he'd used on Wayne Cunningham and a few other patients. What would Sage think if he messed this up? She'd probably wonder why the hell he had anything to say about her own use of magic if he couldn't lift a simple scrap of paper into the air.

It felt like calling his wolf forward, except that he was tapping into a different part of himself. It came in a slow trickle at first, the tiniest tingling of energy through his arms and into his hands. He could sense Sage's eyes on him, which made it that much harder to concentrate. Levitating the streamer up and into place wasn't that hard. It was just the dark feelings that surrounded it. His palms tingled and itched as the crepe paper lifted up and into place.

"Let's do another one!" Sage was ready with the tape. If she'd noticed Dex's hesitation at all, she didn't show it.

The next section was easier. Dex moved his hands in the air, twisting the crepe paper to give it the classic effect just before pushing the tape into place.

"Yay! I like that!"

Suddenly, the decorating was moving along at lightning speed as the two of them worked together. Dex felt himself beginning to relax. A knot of tension and doubt still lingered in his stomach, but he was pushing past it. These were just balloons and streamers, and he and Sage were having a good time.

"Okay, I think that's all of those," he said as they returned to the boxes. "Let's put these table covers on."

It was easier just to unfold the long sheets of plastic and lay them on the tables by hand, but that gave them a nice break from working their magic.

"What about these?" Sage held up a little bag.

It was filled with shiny confetti shaped like pumpkins and leaves. "I'll finish putting the table covers on. Then you can scatter those on the ones that are already done."

"Okay!"

They each went back to work, and Dex was starting to feel that Vanessa would be happy with the results when she got back.

"Daddy! Look!" Sage was holding a handful of the confetti in the air, her arm stretched out. She made a flicking gesture with her left hand, which sent the confetti streaming out along the table.

He hadn't taught her that, and he was pretty sure no one else had, either. "That's very good! You're saving us a lot of time. Have you ever done that before?" Dex tried to sound casual on this last question, not wanting her to know how much it bothered him to see her coming up with new ideas on her own.

"Nope! I just decided to try it. Can I go show Tina? I think we passed her street on the way here."

Absolutely nothing got past this child. "That was the street to the house where her coven lives, but no, I'm afraid we can't do that. Here, look. I found some more confetti. Ghosts and bats."

Sage took the bag from him and occupied herself while he poured bags of candy into apple baskets and set one out on each table.

"I need to go to the bathroom," Sage announced after a while.

"Go out those doors we came in, and it's right across the hall," Dex told her, pointing. He still knew the school like the back of his hand.

Alone in the gym, Dex tried to concentrate on what he was doing. He untangled a large banner made up of individual letters and hung it across the front of the stage on one end of the gym. There was a box of small, inexpensive lanterns. He guessed the tea lights would go inside these, so he went ahead and put one out on each table. Nothing they did was probably what Vanessa had in mind, but even Dex was starting to think it looked pretty good.

His wolf suddenly perked up, restless and agitated. Dex stopped what he was doing and listened to it. Though his mind and body had been entirely out of balance over the last two days, and his wolf might only be stirred up by recent events, he could tell something was off.

Sage.

She hadn't come back from the bathroom. Maybe she'd just needed to take a little extra time in there, but his wolf distinctly sensed she was no longer close by.

Dex pushed through the gym doors. "Sage?"

There was no reply from the girls' bathroom across the hall. He stepped up to the doorway. "Sage? Are you all right?"

There was still no reply.

"I'm coming in there." The building was empty, and he was going to find his daughter. Dex stepped in, but the long row of stalls was empty.

Back in the hall, he jogged around to a few of the

classrooms that were close by. A desperate hope drove him, but he had to face the truth. She wasn't there anymore.

And damn it, he had a good idea of where she'd gone.

Leaving the decorating behind, Dex ran out the front doors. The sun had been setting while they worked to prepare for the party, and it was nearly dark. His wolf fretted. She was too young to be out there alone! "Sage!"

Dex hurried around the corner of the building. Time was of the essence, and he threw caution to the wind as he brought out his wolf. It sprang forward willingly, rippling through his body so fast that it left him a little dizzy as he trotted through the shadows at the side of the school.

Sage's scent was still fresh and distinct, and Dex picked up on it quickly. Just as he'd suspected, she'd headed west. Dex moved quickly, trying to keep in the shadows as much as possible as he headed to the covenstead.

16

The knock on the front door was quiet, but it was enough to make Tina drop the book she'd been reading. It was a Saturday evening, and in an effort to once again not feel sorry for herself, she'd decided to spend it at the covenstead. Not everyone had the chance to sink into the comfort of their first home, and Tina knew how lucky she was.

Retrieving the book from the floor, she set it on the side table and opened the door. "Sage!"

"Hi, Tina!" She smiled up at her as she put her hands behind her back and swiveled back and forth.

"What are you doing here? Not that I'm surprised to see you, but—" She broke off, not wanting to dive into all her private business with

Dex. Tina leaned out the door and looked around. "Where's your dad?"

"He's at the school."

True worry started to creep across Tina's face. This wasn't good. "Does he know you're here?"

She sank her head into her shoulders. "No. I just came to see you because I wanted to show you something I figured out."

Her heart sang at knowing that Sage still wanted to connect with her. Tina hadn't yet figured out how she was going to fulfill her promise to herself to help Sage, but now the sweet little girl was right there on her coven's doorstep.

It was still a problem, though. "As happy as I am to see you, I think your dad is probably worried about you. Let me get my keys, and I'll take you back over there."

"But I really want to show you," Sage whined.

That same whining sound was happening inside Tina. Whatever Sage was excited about, she really wanted to see it. But if Dex didn't know where his daughter was, it was cruel to make him wait another second.

Just then, a wolf padded out of the shadows and into the front yard. Tina's wolf recognized him right away, but she didn't need that fated instinct to have memorized how handsome he was in this form.

Dex phased back into his human form as he reached the edge of the grass and ran up the porch steps. "Sage! There you are! You and I are going to have a talk, young lady."

Tina's eyes darted to the shadows as she caught movement behind Dex. "Who's that?"

Another wolf was approaching, and this one moved swiftly and confidently into the front yard. He zeroed in on Dex with his yellow eyes. Two lanky coyotes flanked him, looking wild and eager.

"Get inside, Sage." Tina stepped aside just as Sage came darting past her, already sensing danger.

The new wolf twisted his head and jerked his shoulders. The coyotes did the same, and a moment later, Chris Kelly and his buddies were walking up to the porch steps. "Dexter Heywood," Chris said in that arrogant, condescending voice of his.

"What the hell are you doing here?" Dex asked.

"Me and my boys were just out on the old field, throwing the pigskin around, when we saw you creeping around the school."

Tina noticed Dex's hands curl into fists. "So you decided to follow me?"

"Hey," Chris said, throwing his palms in the air, "you can't blame me. We weren't all that quiet. You were just a bit distracted."

"Well, I still am. So see you later," Dex asserted.

"No, no," Chris replied with a dry laugh as he took another step closer. "I told you at the reunion that I'd find you and we'd finally settle this score once and for all. And look, now I've found you."

Dex stood his ground even as the trio approached. "I don't have time for your stupid high school bullshit, okay? Why don't you take your buddies and go find something better to do? I'm a little busy."

"Yeah, I see that. Decided to go to the witch's house for some weekend fun." Chris's eyes darted to Tina and raked up and down her body. "Sorry, sweetheart, but your man's got something to take care of. Of course, if you want to be with a real man, maybe we can talk later."

"I wouldn't touch you with a ten-foot pole," she sneered. "Take your mutts and get off my lawn before I call the cops."

"Oh, she's a spicy one," Chris said, looking back at Dex now. "She must be the one who wears the pants in this relationship."

A vein in the side of Dex's neck was throbbing. "You can try all you want to get me riled up, but I'm not fighting you."

"No? Fine." Chris laughed. John and Jacob echoed that laughter, but they stopped as soon as their leader did. "I'm still gonna fight you."

Chris leaped toward Dex, his wolf springing back out of him with swift ferocity. The two of them tumbled backward, knocking Tina aside as they rolled into the house.

"Shit!" Tina hit the floor hard. She thought she saw Sage disappearing up the stairs, grateful for that, at least. She was also thankful that she wasn't the only one home. "Help!"

John, in coyote form, came flying in the door just as Tina was trying to pick herself up off the floor. He bowled her backward, sending her into the wall.

"Now you've really pissed me off!" Tina let her wolf fly free. It'd been wanting out for so long, and it snapped its jaws before it was even fully formed. John was faster in his coyote form, but she was bigger. Shoving her paws beneath her, she shot to her feet and sprang toward him.

Maeve came running into the room from the kitchen, carrying a pan. "What the hell is this?"

"I've got the old lady!" Jacob announced, his last

word cutting off as he let go of his human and returned to four feet. He charged at Maeve.

"Fuck off, fleabag!" Maeve swung back and clocked him hard with the pan.

Jacob let out a yelp as he flew to the side, crashing into the table lamp and then to the floor.

Chelsea came from upstairs. "What's going on? Sage just came running upstairs, and—oh!" She let go of the handrail, her body flying over a few stairs before she landed on all fours. She charged hard into Chris and Dex, who were tangled in a knot of teeth and claws. The force was enough to knock them apart for a moment.

Tina, meanwhile, was still wrestling with John. He was small and wiry, and he didn't look very intimidating, but he was quick. He snapped at her paws and throat as she tried to block him from getting over to Dex. Tina tucked her head and rammed into him. His teeth clamped down hard on her ear as they hit the wall again, and she felt hot blood gushing down the side of her face.

John got back on his paws. He reeled backward, preparing for a hard pounce on her ribs.

Heavy thuds made the floor beneath her shudder. Tina looked up in time to see a bear running in from the back porch.

Amanda roared with anger as she stomped one heavy front paw on the floor. Energy waves radiated from it, and she'd aimed them directly at her target.

John's eyes went wide as he lost his balance and fell on his ass.

Tina was starting to feel pretty good about how this fight was going. Chris and his boys were outnumbered, and they'd been foolish enough to bring the fight to the covenstead. They had no idea just how powerful everyone there could be, nor how much they would sacrifice to save each other and those they cared about.

A deep, ferocious growl had her turning her head, flinging blood against the wall. Chelsea had managed to separate Chris and Dex for a moment, but it hadn't lasted long. Chris had jumped on Dex once again. The two of them were thrashing and biting. Cuts showed as red slashes in their fur, leaving dark stains on the hardwood floor as they rolled further into the room.

Tina saw the flash of Chris's yellow fangs as they sank into Dex's throat. Pure protective rage fueled her as she rushed at him, determined to show this arrogant dick just what a 'little witch' could do.

She bounded through the air, but John's hard skull crashed into her ribs. All the air left her lungs in an instant. The edges of her vision went black, and she felt the heavy impact of the floor. Tina struggled to hold onto consciousness. She couldn't be defeated this easily!

Amanda came after the coyote once again. This time, she wrapped her large mouth around the scruff of his neck and tossed him off to the side. He hit the stair rail and broke two of the spindles, leaving a tuft of bloody coyote fur hanging from one of them.

Meanwhile, Maeve and Jacob were still battling it out. Tina's mother had taken on her stronger wolf form, and she looked pleased with herself as she deftly avoided Jacob's attacks.

Colette came running in the front door. She must have just arrived. She took a quick look around and then opened her palm, instantly summoning a brilliant white sphere of magic. Colette tossed it in the air, and a thin cord of energy kept the orb tied to her hand as she swung it around her head. Her delicate features were hard and determined as she finally let go, letting the sling of magic fly across the room to crash into the side of Jacob's face.

Tina scrambled to her feet once again. Everything was balancing out just fine for most of them, but nothing seemed able to interfere with the two men who were truly at the center of this battle. Chris had told Dex he would settle this fight, but Tina was beginning to worry.

Just how far did he think he had to go before it was over?

17

Dex could taste blood in his mouth, but at this point, he didn't know if it belonged to him or Chris. He was barely aware of the destruction they caused around them as they locked into their fight. Jaws snapped, claws ripped, throats rumbled with growls.

In his mind, though, he was back in the high school gym—not the way it looked right now, half decorated in party supplies, but the way it'd looked twenty-five years ago. As the chaos of the present blurred into the frenzy of the past, the fight replayed itself, starting out of the blue, or at least that's how it felt now:

Chris had just come out of the locker room, cocky and looking for a fight. "I don't like the way you've been looking at me, Heywood." Then, he'd clocked me.

The memory dissolved as Dex felt the weight and push of someone else attacking in the current moment, someone trying to get Chris off of him. It only worked for a second. Chris wouldn't give up. Once he set his mind to something, he'd fight until he got it. Pain from the present brawl drew Dex deeper into the past, where the echoes of shouts and laughter in the gym mingled with the snarls and growls filling the covenstead:

Sharp pain echoed through my face and ribs as Chris pounded me in front of a bunch of other kids at the Academy, but I fought back. I slung my fists and twisted myself, trying to get away. I was strong, but Chris had the advantage of surprise and sheer stupidity.

The illusion shattered when something crashed hard into Dex's back—probably furniture—forcing him to refocus on his opponent. He opened his jaws and snapped, catching Chris's lip. More blood flooded his mouth as his brutal trip down memory lane continued:

I could see the future unfolding in front of me. Chris was already a bully. He picked on anyone and everyone, even those who wisely tried to stay out of his way. Students cowered in fear when he came down the hall. He'd lunge at them, growling, and then he'd laugh when they tried so hard to get away from him that they ran into the lockers. One kid even pissed himself.

Chris's teeth crunched down on Dex's paw, drawing his attention back. Dex reeled as the pain flooded through him. He could feel the bones giving way, the joints snapping. Chris was strong, but he also didn't know when—or how—to stop. That unrelenting brutality dragged Dex's mind back to the gym floor:

I was going to lose, unless I used the one thing Chris didn't have. Fueled by my anger, I let out a burst of magic. It propelled Chris away from me, flinging him across the gym floor. Chris landed on his ass, and the other kids in the gym roared with laughter. His face contorted with hate, Chris got to his feet and barreled across the room. My confidence had grown now. I knew how to defeat him, and it wasn't with punches. I raised my hands and lifted them into the air. Chris cried out as his feet left the ground. "I'll fucking kill you for this!" I only lifted him higher.

A sharp, high-pitched sound brought Dex back to the present moment, a worried whine. Dex's pain was more than just physical—it was in his very soul. It was Tina. They were hurting not just him, but his mate. Her coven was fighting, too, but he was losing. He was losing the same way he had back then, because he'd spent his time living his life instead of focusing only on dominating others. The parallel hit Dex like a kick to the chest, steering his mind back to that moment of fleeting triumph in the gym:

"Okay! Okay!" Chris squealed, flinging his arms and legs helplessly in the air. "I give up. Just put me down!" I felt a rush of victory, but it was quickly vanquished as Mrs. Sharp came bursting into the room, demanding to know what was going on. My concentration slipped, and Chris slammed to the floor. Horror flooded through me, even through my very soul. I'd never meant to kill him.

Shaking off the memory of that atrocity, Dex noted Chris was very much alive now, kicking and stomping with the same relentless fury. Chris leveraged the weight of his body to keep himself on top, never giving Dex the advantage. The yelps and cries from his coyote friends told Dex that they weren't nearly as talented, but Chris was the one who threatened them all the most.

He had to change the balance of this fight. There was plenty of magic all around him. It came from witches who were far more experienced, far more talented, than he could ever be. True fear quivered in his soul. He didn't want to kill anyone.

Tina's words echoed in his mind. Magic was about intention and emotions. If he could keep himself in check, then it wouldn't get out of hand this time. He thought of Sage and how excited she was when Dex had combined his talents with hers. It was a halcyon moment, one that felt like a brief dream of the past, though it'd only just happened that afternoon.

He didn't have his hands to guide his magic. Dex had to do it himself. He had to bring it up from the deepest part of himself, summoning an ancient ability that'd trickled down through his ancestors and had chosen *him*, of all people, to carry it.

Intention.

Was that Tina's voice in his head, or his own?

Dex's magic radiated from him, shoving Chris away. The other wolf rolled across the floor, coming to a stop as he hit a bookshelf. Several volumes tumbled to the ground around him as he stood and shook himself off. He took a step forward and brought his human back out. His face was twisted into that same hate-filled countenance, only older now.

"That's how it's going to be?" Chris demanded. "You won't fight me like a man, so you're going to use your magic on me?"

"It doesn't have to be like this!" Dex hardly even remembered shifting back. He had his hand out and at the ready. He could feel the energy pulsing there, just below the surface of his skin, waiting only for him to send it out into the world.

"You think you're so fucking noble!" Chris started for him again.

"Don't you hurt my Daddy!" Sage cried, running down the stairs.

"Sage, no!" His heart contracted. Time slowed as he watched her little legs charging down the stairs, her hair flying out behind her, her face pinched and angry.

She flung out her hand and swiped it through the air. The coffee table slid across the floor with a screech.

Chris tumbled over it, but his reflexes were quick. He caught himself before he smashed his face on the glass inlay. "What's this, Dex? You're such a fucking wimp that you have to bring a little girl to fight for you?"

A growling bark split through the air as Jacob, still in coyote form, made a flying leap for Sage.

Dex's heart ripped straight out of his chest.

In a flash, a small green dragon came swooping down the stairs, its wings spread and its face fierce. Smoke streamed from its nostrils.

On its back sat a young bobcat, crouching down

and digging its claws in between the dragon's scales as it held on. Its ears were flattened against its head, and its sharp little teeth were bared.

Dex realized this was Corbin in his dragon form, and little Arden as his bobcat. Pure horror ripped through him. It was bad enough that he'd accidentally brought his own fight to the covenstead, but now the children were at risk.

Arden didn't seem to see it that way. The little bobcat coiled on his haunches as Corbin dive-bombed over Jacob. Arden launched off of Corbin's back and landed directly on the coyote's head. He clawed and bit, his screeching hiss muffled because his mouth was full. Tufts of gray fur went flying.

Sparkling green magic quickly lifted the young wildcat into the air. He was still hissing and spitting, swiping uselessly with his fierce little paws as his mother Erin brought him back to safety.

It all happened so quickly, but Dex was already on his way. He wasn't about to let anything happen to Sage. Chris was there for him, but he abandoned that fight to protect his daughter. He dove for Jacob.

To his surprise, so did Chris. The two wolves slammed into him at the same time, knocking him back down to the floor. Chris brought his jaws down on Jacob's throat, growling and snarling until Jacob yipped in submission.

As quickly as it'd begun, the fight was over. The orbs and sparks of magic instantly dissipated. John shifted back into his human form and put his hands in the air. "We're cool, we're cool," he kept repeating. Amanda stood watch over him, making him twitch whenever her bear's hot breath reached him.

Jacob was also a human again, though he was still on the floor.

"What the hell?" Chris asked him, getting up. "Why would you go after a little girl?"

"Dude, I was just being your backup," Jacob protested. "I don't know."

Dex left the two of them. He scooped Sage up in his arms and held her tightly. "Are you okay, baby? Are you all right?"

"I'm fine, Daddy. What about you?" She touched the fresh scar along the side of his neck.

"Don't you worry about me." The scar had been a deep gash a moment ago, but his shifter genes were already healing it quickly. By the next day, even that pink line would be gone.

He turned to Tina, who was hovering nearby with tears in her eyes. "Is she all right?"

"What about you?" His wolf was still very present

within him, and it urged him to reach out and pull her into his embrace. Dex stood there for a moment, holding Sage and Tina and trying to absorb the fact that they'd all lived through this nightmare.

"Get him out of here," Chris was commanding John. "I'll deal with him later."

"I'm really sorry," Jacob muttered as John grabbed him by the back of the collar and led him out of the house.

"I'm not really into curses, but I'm sure I could come up with one," Maeve said, glaring after him.

"Dexter."

He turned to look at Chris. For the first time, his high school foe looked truly remorseful.

"I—I hardly know what to say." His voice was quiet, and Dex thought he saw Chris's hand shaking as he swiped it through his hair. "I'm horrified it went that far. It's one thing to fight man-to-man, but a kid...That wasn't okay."

"I think my Sisters and I should take the kids into the kitchen to get a bite to eat," Tina said, reaching out hopefully for Sage.

She lunged into Tina's arms. "Do you have any cookies?"

"I think we can find some," Tina promised as she moved past Dex toward the kitchen.

The other witches followed. Chelsea was giving Corbin an earful. "I've told you not to use your dragon in the house. Before you know it, you'll be far too big. And what were you thinking, getting involved, anyway? You could've been seriously hurt!"

"It was Arden's idea," Corbin protested. "He said we needed to protect Sage."

"We did a good job of it, too," Arden added. "Did you see me, Mom? The way I ripped his fur out? It was awesome!"

Erin pressed her finger and thumb to her forehead. "We've got a lot to talk about, Arden."

Amanda and Maeve exchanged amused glances as they followed the others.

That left Dex alone with Chris.

18

Dex rested his hand on the newel post. It'd survived the battle, but it wiggled at his touch. His eyes traced the railing upward to the broken spindles and the splatters of blood on the carpet. The more he looked, the more blood he found. Drops of it had been flung like paint against the wall. The area rug closest to the door was dark with it, a mix of his own blood and Chris's.

Chris took a deep breath. "I really am sorry, Dex. I wanted to fight you, but I never meant for anyone else to get involved—especially kids." He cast a worried glance over his shoulder at the kitchen door. "Do you think they're all right?"

"As much as they can be, after seeing that," Dex replied soberly. Anger still roiled in his blood, but it wasn't the kind that could be solved with a punch. "I never wanted a rematch, you know. I tried to tell you at the reunion. I tried to tell you here. I don't have the time or space in my life to go throwing fists, especially for no good reason."

"No good reason?" Chris snapped, and for a moment, his fists curled once again. His shoulders tensed, and a bit of that rage Dex had seen on his face so often came back. Then he huffed out a breath and relaxed. "It felt like there was plenty of reason to me."

Dex turned and sat on the staircase. "Not to me. I've been spending my whole life trying to put that fight behind me. That was a day I never wanted to live through again. As hard as I tried, I couldn't forget about it."

"Yeah, well, me neither." Chris leaned against the open door and looked out into the night. "That was why I wanted to do it again, though."

"I don't get it." Dex studied his rival. When Chris wasn't trying so hard to impress everyone else, he was just a regular guy.

"You wouldn't." Chris shook his head and stepped onto the porch. "Maybe I should just go."

"If you do, you should know I'm not doing this again. We're not going to run into each other again in twenty years and start throwing fists. If there's something we need to work out, we can do it right now. With words."

Chris licked his lip and then sucked it in with his teeth. He hesitated in the doorway, clearly torn.

"I might understand more than you think," Dex told him. He and Chris would never be friends, no matter how much they tried to work things out. But if this was a chance for them to finally put the past to rest, he wanted to take advantage of it. For his sake. For Sage's.

After a moment, Chris began. "I wanted to put that fight behind me. I was pissed about it while I was recovering, angry that I could actually be wounded that badly. I blamed you. I blamed my parents. I blamed the school. Everyone.

"And then I just wanted to forget about it and pretend it'd never happened. I mean, me, the top jock in the whole school and—let's face it—pretty much all of Salem, had been brought to his knees. That just wasn't cool. That wasn't how things were supposed to go. It embarrassed the shit out of me."

"Enough to want to do it all over again?" Dex asked quietly.

"I knew you wouldn't get it." Chris threw his hands in the air in frustration, but he didn't leave.

"See, everything else that happened in my life went back to that fight. Every negative thing that I experienced was all because of one single day."

Everything feels big when you're a teenager, even when it doesn't matter all that much in the long run. That was why schools were filled with so much unnecessary drama. Dex kept that to himself, though. He wanted Chris to talk.

Chris took a step back into the house. "I was a hell of a football player. I was at my absolute peak of physical conditioning. I healed physically after that fight—pretty quickly, thanks to my wolf—but I didn't really recover. I got depressed. I mean, I didn't realize that's what it was at the time, but I can see it now. I didn't want to do anything. Everything just got kind of meaningless.

"I couldn't keep up with my grades. I started missing classes. Some scouts had come to the school earlier in the season, and I'd been promised a sizeable scholarship to a good school, and all I had to do was play football and get good grades. I lost out on that."

Dex vaguely remembered hearing that Chris was going to play for some university, but he'd never checked to see if that had happened.

"My parents talked me into going to North Shore

and at least getting a start on my education. There's nothing wrong with community colleges, but it wasn't what I *wanted*." He curled his hand in the air as though something had just slipped out of his grasp. "It wasn't what I felt I was supposed to be doing. I didn't last long, and I dropped out. I had a few jobs here and there, but they were dead ends. They weren't going anywhere, and neither was I.

"So, I ended up working for my uncle. I think he just felt sorry for me." Chris's head drooped. "Hell, I feel sorry for myself most of the time. I'm not in a good place, Dex, and it all goes back to that one day."

Dex waited a moment, giving Chris's story space and time. His throat was raw from the fight. His joints were achy. He longed to get Sage back in his arms so he could promise he'd always protect her. But he had to do this before he did anything else.

"My life since then hasn't followed the same path, Chris, but I've been affected more than you might think—more than I want to admit most of the time."

Dex closed his eyes. The images had flashed through his mind during the battle, and they were still so fresh. "My grandma was the only other person in my family with magical abilities. She told me to be careful with them. Like any teen who thinks they know everything already, I just promised her I would and moved on.

"I never would've used them against another person, but I felt desperate. Cornered. I felt like I was dying. I wanted to teach you a lesson. All of that is true, but it's not really an excuse." That was the thing about magic. Even if it felt justified, there was always a price to pay. "I only dropped you because I lost my concentration. I never meant for it to get that far."

Though Dex hadn't been sure he would, Chris seemed to really be listening. "I didn't know that."

"I thought I'd killed you," Dex choked out. He'd said those words to friends and family when it came up, but he'd never said them to Chris himself. "It changed something inside me. It made me determined to make up for it. That's why I went into emergency services. If I could save lives, maybe I wasn't a killer after all."

Chris scoffed. "That doesn't seem like such a bad thing. At least you have a real job, one with responsibility and respect."

"Yes," Dex acknowledged, "but I also stopped using magic almost entirely. I didn't trust myself with it anymore. I didn't want to have anything to do with it, especially if I was only going to cause more harm than good."

Walking over to the coffee table, which was still out of place in the pathway of the room, Chris nudged the heavy leg of it with his foot. "You must not have given it up completely. That little girl of yours is pretty talented."

"That's not all thanks to me." Dex frowned as he thought about Tina and Sage and the connection the two of them had. "I've made a lot of mistakes."

"I see." Chris nodded. He was silent for a moment, still bumping the toe of his shoe against the coffee table. Then he looked up. "How about we call a truce?"

"No." Dex got up from the stairs and came to stand in front of Chris. "Not a truce, because that means the fighting is just going to start up again. How about an end to this instead? I say we truly bury the hatchet and leave all this in the past where it belongs."

Chris stuck out his hand. "Agreed."

Dex shook it, and as he did, he felt a weight lifted from his shoulders. "Too bad we couldn't have talked all this out in the first place."

"I don't know that I would've been willing to," Chris admitted. "It was the kids getting involved that really made me wake up and see what was going on. You and I were just kids, and we let one day run our lives. I don't want that to happen to anyone else."

Dex's gut hollowed out. Chris was absolutely right, of course. They couldn't base their whole future on one incident. But was he trying to base Sage's future on something that happened to him long before she was even born? "Me, neither."

"I'll get out of here, but again, I really am sorry. If there's anything I can do, just let me know."

"Okay." Dex glanced at the kitchen door. "I've got to go make some apologies of my own, though."

"I'll see you around, Dex." Chris paused as he turned toward the door. "It looks like you need a good construction company. I know a guy." He brushed his fist against Dex's upper arm and walked out the door.

The battle was over, but the rest of the war had yet to be settled. Dex steeled himself for something much harder than a physical fight or even a magical one. He pushed through the kitchen door.

All the witches looked up at him in an instant. They'd said they were going to make some snacks for the kids, but it looked like they'd emptied the entire contents of the fridge onto the kitchen table. The children ate ravenously even as they gave him curious looks, undoubtedly exhausted from the fight.

"Is everything all right?" Maeve asked carefully.

"Yes. Chris and the others are gone. I'll pay for all the damages. I'm truly sorry that this happened the way it did."

Maeve gave him a generous nod. "Would you like anything to eat?"

"No, thank you." His wolf said otherwise after having an evening like that. Dex walked to the table and looked at Corbin, Arden, and Sage. "I'm sorry that you kids had to see that, and I'm doubly sorry that you felt the need to join in. That fight was my responsibility, and I never meant to bring it here. You were very brave, but I don't like the idea that you could've been seriously injured."

The boys didn't seem too phased by it, but Erin nodded her approval. "It's given us the opportunity to have some very long and thorough talks with them."

"And Sage." He would probably have some long and thorough talks with her, too, but this one wouldn't wait. He'd already wasted enough time. "There are times when we should use our magic, and there are times when we shouldn't. It's not always easy to tell the difference. I want to make sure you continue to get proper training so that you'll never have to question yourself."

"With Tina?" Sage asked hopefully.

His eyes drifted to Tina, who was sitting next to Sage with a protective arm around the back of her chair. She gave him a solemn nod.

"Yes." He never thought it would feel so good to tell her that. "With Tina. And with me, too."

"Yay!" She had piles of various food on her plate, and she waved a chip in the air in celebration. "Can we stay for a little while longer, Daddy? Maeve said she had some chocolate cake for us."

"Indeed, I do," Maeve replied benevolently. "Such ferocious warriors deserve no less."

"Mom," Chelsea chastised.

"What?" Maeve was already heading to the fridge to fetch the cake.

Dex met Tina's gaze again. "Could I talk to you? Alone?"

"Sure." She got up from the table and walked with him through the kitchen door. She made a face as she took in the chaos of the living room, with its broken furniture and ruined walls. "Maybe not in here, though."

Instead, they stepped out the front door and down the walkway, a short distance from the house.

Dex looked up at it. With its rows of windows, many of which had a welcoming glow, the covenstead wasn't unlike his own packhouse. It was a place for respite, for growth, for comfort. He felt guilty all over again.

"Tina, I owe you an apology. Actually, I owe you a whole string of them," he began. "I'll probably think of a few more things to apologize for after I get home, too."

She let out a soft laugh. "That's just how the last couple of weeks have been, right?"

"Definitely." There really was so much he wanted to fix between them. This part was the hardest and the one that dominated his mind the most. "I truly am sorry for the way I treated you in your store. I'm appalled that I spoke to you that way, and that I completely dismissed what you had to say."

She watched him with tired eyes. "That's all right."

Dex wondered if the separation between them had dug down into her soul the same way that it had his. "No. It's not all right. I overreacted. I was so worried about Sage's emotional state and the harm she might cause, but the truth is that I needed to look in the mirror. I need to work on my emotional state when it comes to magic, and especially my history with magic. Holding out on Sage's education wasn't helping her. It was just something that made me feel better in the moment."

"I understand."

"You do?" He felt his wolf reacting to her presence, just as it always had. It told him to grab her and pull her close, to kiss her like he'd never kissed anyone before, to hold her tightly and never let go. It told him he was the biggest fool in Salem if he thought he could ever make it without her.

But the cool distance of her eyes told him otherwise. He'd done some real damage, and his actions had caused distance between them.

"I do," she affirmed. "It took me some time and a little help to see it, but you were just trying to put Sage first. You're a good father, and you only want what's best for her. I just wish you understood that's what I want, too."

"I know it now," he admitted. "That's exactly why I asked if you'd continue training her, despite her father being a complete ass every now and again. I probably should've asked you privately before I said anything in front of her, but—"

"But you figured I'd say yes anyway?" she concluded for him. "I would. In fact, I was hoping to find some way to help her, in spite of you and me being at odds. I wonder if that makes me a bad person for wanting to butt in on a child's life when I'm not their parent, but I can't help it. Sage is a very special little girl."

"Then we have at least one thing we agree on." He hoped that someday it would be more, that at some point they could at least look at each other without such wariness. "So you really will continue training her?"

"Yes. Does Monday night work?"

"I'm sure it does." He had no idea what was on his calendar for Monday, especially after all they'd just been through, but he would make it happen, no matter what.

"Great. Then I'll be there."

19

"I WANT YOU TO CLOSE YOUR EYES AND TRY TO CLEAR your mind," Tina instructed gently as she lit the last candle. Sage's lessons were taking place in the guest bedroom at Dex's house. The space was calm and peaceful, and they could close the door. It also meant that the lessons would be a little easier on Sage's schedule and give her more time for being a child instead of just being schlepped around from one event to the next.

Tina felt that last part was crucial. Sage could find a passion and work hard toward it, but she also needed time to simply be a kid.

The bonus was that Sage could set up her very own altar right there in the spare room. She kneeled in front of the old wooden chest right now. It was covered with a soft scarf, a special present from Maeve. A framed photo of Marie sat in the very center, and Tina had given Sage free rein to arrange flowers, crystals, kid-friendly candles, and anything else that pleased her around it.

"How do you clear your mind?" Sage asked, opening one eye.

"It's a challenge," Tina admitted. "Our thoughts can be very busy. You have to try not to think about anything at all for a short time. When you think you've done the very best that you can, say the words we went over."

"Okay." Sage sounded a little uncertain, but she closed her eyes again and took a deep breath.

There was a long, meditative silence. Tina also closed her eyes and absorbed the peace there between the two of them. As much as she loved running The Crystal Cauldron, it was coming there two days a week to teach Sage that truly made her happy.

"Mommy," Sage said softly, "I want you to look out for me and guide me. I also want to see you again, if I can."

Tina opened her eyes to watch as Sage did the same. The little girl picked up the small, round mirror on her altar and held it before her eyes. It flashed and shimmered.

Sage smiled. She tipped her head slightly to the side, and she nodded as though she were listening. Her face changed slightly, and then she smiled again, setting the mirror down.

"Well?" Tina asked.

"I saw her!" Sage nearly shouted. "I wasn't sure I would since it isn't Samhain anymore, but she was still there!" She wrapped her arms around Tina.

Her heart and spirit were in pure bliss. Tina had known all the way down in the center of her gut that Marie had reached out to Sage on Samhain not as a simple hello, but as one of her spirit guides. Who better to be a contact from the other side? "I'm so happy for you, sweetheart."

Sage turned her head and rested her cheek on Tina's shoulder. "She told me that she loves me. She said that she knows I miss her, but that I don't need to because she's right here with me all the time."

"That's so wonderful." Tina ran her hand down Sage's long, curly hair. "And she's absolutely right. You can reach out to her any time you need, and she'll always be there."

"Do you know what else she said?" Sage asked.

"No. Would you like to tell me?" Though it was

Tina's job to teach as much as she could to Sage, some things were very private. Sage's conversations with her spirit guides—whether with Marie or anyone else—weren't her business.

Sage pulled back so she could look Tina in the face. "She wanted me to tell you something."

Tina swallowed and tried not to let the shock register on her face. It was unusual for a spirit guide to deliver a message intended for someone else. "What's that, honey?"

"She said to say thank you." Sage shrugged. "I don't know for what. That's all she said."

"That's all right." Now Tina had to fight back the tears that burned the backs of her eyes. "I understand. It looks like it's about time for us to wrap up for today. Do you remember how to close down your altar?"

"Yep!" Sage bounced off her lap and began methodically turning off her LED candles, thanking any spirits who came to aid her.

Tina used that moment to compose herself. Dex had asked her to teach Sage, and she'd been more than happy to resume the role. They'd been working together for several weeks now, and every day, Sage's powers and intuition seemed to grow. Dex seemed appreciative, always politely thanking her. Sage greeted her at the door every day with a smile, always asking her questions or showing her what she'd been practicing. Tina knew she was valued.

But to know that even Marie approved of her and what she was doing for Sage meant so much. To hear those two simple words, spoken through Sage, moved her deeply. A mother's love was strong and powerful, and so was her acceptance.

The doorbell rang as Sage and Tina emerged from the spare room. "It's Aunt Debbie!" Sage announced, running to answer it. "We're going to a party!"

"You certainly do love those," Tina murmured.

Sage opened the door. Savannah and Colton came running in, with their mother trailing in shortly after.

Debbie beamed at Tina. "Hey! We didn't get here too early and interrupt your lesson, did we?"

"No, not at all. We just finished up," Tina told her. She'd never gotten to know Debbie all that well while they'd been in school together. Lately, however, Debbie had been coming around a bit when Tina was still at the house and taking a little time to chat. Tina was finding that she really enjoyed her company.

Debbie watched as the kids ran down the hall to

Sage's room. "Listen, I just want to tell you how wonderful all of this is."

"What do you mean?"

"What you're doing for Sage," Debbie clarified, lowering her voice a bit. "It's the lessons, sure, but it's so much more than that. Sage has always been a pretty bright and happy kid, and she seemed to deal with Marie's death pretty well. Almost too well, really. But now I see a real difference in her, and I think it's thanks to you."

"That's very kind of you. I do my best, but I could never take the place of her mother."

"No," Debbie said hesitantly, "but I think you've earned a pretty darn special place in her life." She winked.

Dex walked in from the kitchen. "What are you two conspiring about?"

"Not a thing." Debbie straightened up and called down the hall. "Kids! We'd better go, or we'll be late for the party!"

Sage, Savannah, and Colton came barreling back out into the living room. Sage hugged Tina and then her father before following her cousins out the door. Debbie followed the whirlwind, pausing to give them a finger wave before she left. "A whole night of kids eating cake at a trampoline park. Wish me luck that no one pukes!"

When the door closed, Tina went to get her purse off the side table where she'd left it. "Sounds like you get a nice, peaceful evening at home. Unless you have to work, that is."

"Later I do, but do you have time to stay for a bit? I'd like to talk to you about something."

Her stomach trembled, but she forced it to calm down. "Sure. I've got a minute."

"Have a seat. I'll pour us each a glass of wine." Dex disappeared into the kitchen before she could protest.

Tina sat on the couch, still trying to settle her nerves.

Dex returned a moment later with two glasses of wine and handed her one. He sat down next to her. "I want to thank you."

It was a night for that, apparently. Tina sipped her drink—Moscato, her new favorite. "You don't have to thank me. I'm really happy to do this. Sage means a lot to me, and I enjoy seeing her abilities blossom." At this point in her life, Tina would probably never have children of her own. Her experiences with Sage, however, satisfied something very deep within her.

"It's that," Dex said, staring down into his glass, "but it's a lot more."

"What do you mean?" Tina took another sip. She wasn't as nervous now, but her wolf was churning inside her, being so close to him. If she just turned a little further to her right, their knees would touch.

"You fought for her," he said, a catch in his voice. "You put your life on the line that night that Chris showed up at the covenstead. You also fought with me on her behalf, for her right to continue her education. That says a lot about you."

Tina shook her head dismissively. "It's what anyone would've done."

"No, it isn't. I think you know that. *I* know that." He put down his glass. "Tina, it's hard being a single parent for many reasons. I worried about bringing a woman into Sage's life, but I've realized that I only really needed to worry about bringing in the right one."

Her throat was tight, and her wolf was standing at attention.

Dex took her free hand. "The right one is you, and it always has been. I love you, Tina. I know I haven't done a very good job of showing it, not at any point, but I'd like to change that. I'm hoping you might forgive me for being an anxious fool."

She eyed him carefully. He was so handsome, but it wasn't just his dazzling eyes or the lines of his features that pierced her. It was the fierceness with which he loved. He'd made some mistakes, yes, but it was only because he cared so much. "You want to try again?"

"I really do." His fingers tightened around hers. "I've proven to myself that I can live without you, but I don't want to."

It was hard to look at him and find the boy she'd come to know as a teenager. He was different now. Experience had hardened him, but not his heart. She loved him. She'd always loved him, and that love had grown and changed over the years, just as they had. "I don't want to live without you either, Dex. Not without you or Sage. It's been hard to come here every week, spend time with the two of you, and pretend that it's nothing more."

Dex picked his glass back up and held it in front of him. "To a new future."

"And a rather bright one," she added. As they clinked glasses and she took another sip, Tina looked up over the rim. Her stomach was in knots, but ones of anticipation for all that was to come.

He pulled her close and kissed her, his lips tasting sweetly of wine.

Somehow, she managed to put her glass back on the coffee table as she kissed him back. Every muscle in her body relaxed as she pressed her lips against his, falling into the sweet comfort of truly finding her mate. How many times had she left his place, wishing she could kiss him goodbye?

Now she could kiss him whenever she wanted, and she was more than ready to take advantage of that. Her body thrilled as they wrapped their arms around each other, no longer needing to keep a distance between them. She'd only had a few sips of wine, but she was buzzed from having her mate in her arms.

Tina never wanted to let him go again, and she was determined to show him that. She parted her lips as she kissed him, inspiring him to do the same. She slipped her tongue into his mouth, twining it with his, relishing the texture as she claimed him.

Her hands reached up, cupping his jaw and gliding over the planes of his face. She wanted to know the touch of him, the feel of him, to understand the connection between their bodies, no matter if she was using her lips, her hands, or any other part of her.

It was the bond between their souls, however, that truly drove her desire. Tina could sense his wolf, tapping into it almost as easily as she could her own. The beasts were nearly tame after running feral and detached for so long, pining and searching, but never really finding what they were looking for.

It was all there now.

Tina put her leg over Dex, spreading her thighs over his lap as she continued to kiss him. Already, she could feel his hardness stirring against her. She rolled her hips forward and up, gently grinding against him.

Dex moaned into her mouth, a pleasant vibration that took her excitement up another notch, along with the way he slid his hands down her back until he cupped her backside. He massaged her curves, encouraging her and the way she moved against him.

Tina came up for a breath. "I love the way you touch me," she whispered.

"I'm more than happy to oblige." He kissed the hollow of her collarbone and then trailed his lips downward. Dex pulled the square neck of her knit top down, revealing her bra. He kissed the exposed tops of her breasts and then dipped his tongue down inside the cups.

Heat flooded through her. That sweet tension was beginning to rise inside her, increasing as she continued to rock against the hardness in his jeans. Her fingers were entwined around the back of his neck, stroking the cords of muscle and the freshly cropped hair.

She was just about to take off her shirt when Dex's arms wrapped tight and hard around her. He surged up from the couch, easily lifting both their weights.

Tina squealed in surprise and pulled her arms around his neck. She enveloped his hips with her legs, although he was holding her up just fine on his own. "Where are we going?" she asked breathlessly.

Dex walked around the couch. "I'm going to bed you properly this time."

Those words sent another tingling jolt through her body. "Does that mean you couched me last time?" she teased.

He growled as he turned, pressing her up against the wall. Dex held her in place with only the pressure of his hips, leaving his hands free to roam her body. He kissed her hungrily, almost desperately, his stubble leaving her skin raw around her mouth. His hands ran over her thighs and ribs, along her arms and in her hair. "Bed tonight," he promised as his kisses wandered down her throat. "After that, maybe here, the hallway, the middle of the woods."

Intrigue swirled inside her. His erection was throbbing against her core, and she could hardly stand the fact that clothes still separated them. "Where else?" she panted, fantasizing about their bodies tumbling together through the leaves.

Dex found the front clasp of her bra and nuzzled her bare breasts. "The shower," he replied without hesitation. "Hot, steamy, soapy."

Her breaths were coming more quickly now as she imagined water running down his body, his hands gliding lather over hers. He had her breast in his mouth, and as his tongue rapidly flicked her nipple, she felt an echoing reaction between her legs. "Tell me more," she gasped. "Where else?"

He pulled back slightly, arching a brow at her. "In the back of your store?" He traced a slow, heated circle around her nipple with his tongue.

It was absolutely wrong to snatch a quick moment with him after hours, which made it all the more appealing. "You're going to make me come just talking about it."

"Then imagine how good it'll be when we actually do all those things." He put his arms under her and pulled her off the wall. He carried her down to the end of the hall and kicked open the door. "But for tonight, the bedroom."

They tumbled onto the bed together, frantically kissing as they pulled off their clothes. Tina whipped off her shirt and squirmed out of her bra. She sighed as Dex took off his shirt, revealing his broad chest, strong shoulders, and tight abs.

She pushed him back against the pillows and opened his jeans. Next came his boxer briefs. She ran her finger down the thin trail of hair that started at his navel and led her straight to what she really wanted.

Tina straddled his muscular thighs. She wrapped her hand around his shaft and stroked slowly, gliding her fingers over the soft skin, teasing him, enticing him.

She lifted her hips and sank down on top of him. Dex put his hands on her waist and pulled himself against her, tightening their connection until they couldn't be any closer.

She braced her hands on his chest and dipped down slowly, moving her body against his, his heated shaft filling her. With her legs spread, her most sensitive spot throbbed. His words had already gotten her halfway there, and it didn't take long before their speed increased, both of them building into a frenzy of desire, passion, and the knowledge that they were truly meant to be together.

He was her mate. Hers. For the rest of their lives.

The coil of tension that'd been turning tighter and tighter finally released. Tina cried out as her body spasmed, pleasure blooming from her core and radiating outward. Dex's hands clamped hard around her hips, deep groans vibrating from his chest with each thrust until neither of them could take any more.

Panting, she kissed him once again.

She lay next to him in the dark, her head resting on his chest. Tina listened to the steady thrum of his heart, and she felt her own beating in a steady reply. She was happy and content, purely satisfied, but she sensed a certain tension in him. "What is it?" she asked into the darkness.

He moved away from her slightly so that he could turn on the bedside lamp. "There's something I want to ask you."

"I thought you already asked me," she teased.

Dex laughed lightly and kissed her forehead. "No, something else."

She wasn't nervous this time. The two of them were going to face the world together. Everything would be all right, no matter what. She propped herself up on one elbow to look at him, still safe in the crook of his arm.

"You're a big part of Sage's life, and you're about to be an even bigger part now that we're together." His thumb made slow arcs against her lower back. "Would you be Sage's legal guardian and magical custodian?"

"Oh, Dex!" After the pleasure they'd felt together in bed, Tina had no control over her emotions. Tears dripped down her cheeks and onto his chest. "Me? Really?"

"Who else would it be?" He pulled her close and kissed her tears away. "What do you say?"

"Yes," she cried. "Absolutely, yes."

EPILOGUE

"How did this get to be so big?" Dex asked, nervously looking around as more and more of the Heywood pack arrived at the covenstead. "I thought we were just going to have a small ceremony."

David put his arm around his son's shoulders and hugged him tightly. "Consider it a blessing! Everyone wanted to be here. It says a lot about you and Sage, and about Tina, too."

"I know you're right. It's just...I don't know. I'm a little nervous. But it's not like I have cold feet," Dex quickly corrected. "I know this is what I want."

"I know that, too," his father assured him, "otherwise you wouldn't be doing it. And it's all right. Everyone gets a little nervous when they have to stand up in front of dozens of people and declare their feelings."

"Not helping," Dex said flatly.

Joyce appeared next to them, grinning. "I think everyone is here! We're ready to get started. Tina and Sage are waiting for you on the back porch. Everyone else is in the yard."

"All right." It was all going by so quickly. Though it was a lot to have almost his entire pack and Tina's whole coven all in one spot, Dex was glad. Everyone they knew would get to see how much they loved each other.

As he stepped out onto the porch, he found Tina crouching down in front of Sage, giving her dress and hair the final touches. She stood, and he could see the long purple gown that flattered her brown eyes. The cloak attached at the shoulders gave her a regal look.

"Daddy!" Sage said when she saw him. She twirled in a circle, making the pink skirt of her dress puff out. "Do you like my dress? Tina helped me pick it out!"

"Yes, I do. It's very lovely." His eyes roved back to Tina, completely entranced by her. How lucky was he to have a woman this beautiful in his life? "You both do."

"Shall we?" Tina asked.

The music struck up outside, filtering easily into the screen porch. "It sounds like it."

They stepped outside onto the little walkway. Dex held out his arm for Tina and his hand for Sage. The three of them walked around the corner of the house and into the backyard, where all their friends and family were waiting for them. His nerves turned to pride as he escorted his two favorite people into their future.

Numerous rows of chairs had been assembled to accommodate all their guests. Candles stood at intervals around the yard, with greenery twined around their tall stands. It was chilly, but the small bonfire that crackled nearby promised a good chance to warm up after the nuptials. Friends and family beamed at them as they walked toward Maeve, who waited under an arch of cedar boughs.

The High Priestess waited until the music stopped. Her eyes were soft and happy as she looked at them, and then past them at the audience. "Friends and family, today we've come together to share in the celebration of our loved ones, to make official something that has been true for a very long time in their hearts. I thank you for allowing me to be a part of it.

"Today, we bind together not just a couple, but a family. Through you, all of us here are also bound as we share in your love and commitment. Please take each other's hands."

Dex turned so that he faced Tina. Sage stood between them, facing Maeve. Dex put out his hand, and Sage put hers on top. Her little fingers wiggled against Dex's knuckles. Tina's hand was last, covering them both.

Savannah and Colton stepped forward to hand Maeve a complicated cord. It'd taken Tina hours to make this witch's thread, composed of parts of their lives. It was woven with Tina's hair and Dex's wolf fur. Sage had made a contribution as well, with the pink moonstone necklace Dex had bought for her on that fateful day when they'd wandered into Tina's shop.

Maeve wound the cord carefully around their hands. "This is a symbol of all the ties that already bind you. You've been brought together here on Earth because your souls already knew each other on another plane. This cord reminds you that you shall forever be entwined." Her fingers deftly tied a knot just under their hands, leaving the two ends and a loop dangling. "It is my privilege to accompany you on this journey, but only you can tie the knot of your fate."

Dex's eyes met Tina's, and he knew he'd be happy to look into those same eyes every morning for the rest of his life. Her smile told him that she felt the same way.

He looked down at Sage. "Are you ready?"

She nodded eagerly.

Dex and Tina each took one end of the cord, and Sage held the loop. They all removed their hands and pulled on their section of the cord. The coils that'd been around their hands twisted and turned, forming a tight knot at the very center. A glowing pulse of magic radiated from the knot and touched each one of them.

"So shall it be," Maeve intoned.

"So shall it be!" the guests called back eagerly, followed by applause, shouts, and cheers.

Dex kissed Tina, smiling at the whistles that came from his cousins. "I love you. I love both of you."

"I love you, too," she replied, looking content.

"Are we a family now?" Sage asked.

A few of the guests laughed.

"We are."

The reception began immediately afterward.

Guests carried mugs of hot cider or cocoa. Chafing dishes held loads of delicious food, including Dex's white chili. No one seemed to mind the cold, and the most susceptible among them stayed near the bonfire. That worked perfectly, since the elders so enjoyed watching the children make s'mores. It took quite some time, but Dex and Tina managed to work their way through all of the guests, thanking them all for coming and accepting their warm wishes.

"That was exhausting," Dex said with a smile as they slipped around the corner of the house for a quick moment alone.

"Yes, but a good kind of exhausting," she agreed.

"I think the best kind of exhausting is going to come later tonight, back at the house." He pulled her close and nuzzled her neck. "As good as you look in that dress, I think you'll look even better when I get the chance to take it off of you."

Her hands roved up his arms, around his shoulders, and along the base of his neck. "That sounds like the perfect chance to warm up after this long day outside."

"First, we have to get rid of these guests." He inhaled the sweet scent of her perfume as he traced her hips with his thumbs.

"No, we don't," she said with a deep-throated

laugh. "It's not our house. We can just slip away whenever we want to."

"Dex? Tina?" Joyce's voice lifted above the din in the yard. "Your Aunt Rita wants to see you again before she leaves."

Dex braced his head against Tina's shoulder. "I guess we'll have to wait a little longer."

They returned to their guests, getting plenty more hugs from Aunt Rita. Then they found Sage standing by herself near the back fence. Her head was tipped up, and she had her back turned to the house.

"Sage?" Dex asked. "Is everything okay?"

"Look," she said softly.

A tiny chickadee was hopping along the top of the fence. It sang to Sage in its little two-note song, one high and one low, seemingly indifferent to the crowd gathered there. After a moment, it fluttered into the air, zooming not far over Sage's head before it shot up into the trees and disappeared. A single feather drifted down from it, landing perfectly in Sage's outstretched hand.

"It was Mommy," Sage explained as she turned to her parents. "She wanted to tell me how happy she is."

Dex saw tears in Tina's eyes and had to look away before they spread to his. "I think we all are."

THE END

If you enjoyed Tina and Dex's story, read on for a preview of Amanda and Lars's story, *Fated Midlife Christmas*!

AMANDA AND LARS

"Wow. This is a huge turnout," Amanda Quinn observed as she threaded her way through the crowd along Washington Square. Throngs of people were already lining up across the street from the Hawthorne Hotel. For early December, downtown Salem was unusually packed—busier, even, than it always was on Halloween. A brass band played nearby, and several vendor stalls had been set up along the street. Adults chatted while children tipped their heads back, staring up hopefully at the roof of the iconic building.

"What do you expect?" her cousin Kristy asked, her green eyes bright beneath her knit hat. For once, she wasn't fiddling with a deck of tarot or oracle cards. "It's not every day you get to see Santa arrive."

"How long until he comes?" Sage asked, bouncing along as she held Tina's hand. Her long locks had been carefully tamed into two braids, each tied with sparkling red ribbons at the end.

"Soon, I think. We've just got to find Aunt Chelsea and Uncle Beck. They're supposed to already be here with Corbin," Tina explained patiently. She lifted her head and looked through the crowd.

"Who was it that they said was coming?" Erin asked, rubbing a smearing of peanut butter and jelly off Arden's chin. "I know Chelsea told me, but I've been a bit busy at the shop. Everyone wants holiday herbal teas, and I've been crafting some new ones for this year."

"Someone that Beck knows," Kristy replied. She reached absently into her pocket and pulled out a deck of cards. She looked at her gloved hands, frowned, and put the deck back. "From Norway, I think?"

"Those dragons really do get around," Tina remarked.

Amanda smiled to herself. It was only in a place like Salem where you could mention a supernatural being in the middle of a crowd and not have anyone look at you sideways. By her appearance, no one would know that she could shift into a bear at any moment, nor that she could do magic, but the same was likely true of plenty of others in the crowd.

Sirens split the air as a fire truck slowly pulled up in front of the hotel, its lights flashing. Children began screaming, knowing that the special moment was getting closer.

Arden was starting to get really excited now. "A fire truck! A fire truck!"

Amanda looked around as they moved along South Washington Square. "I don't see Chelsea anywhere."

"Hang on. I just got a text." Tina fished her phone out of her pocket. "She and Beck went to get some cocoa for Corbin. They were right near the entrance to the Commons, so we can just meet up with them when they get back."

Fortunately, there was still some room on the circle of brick pavers right at the corner of the street, so the group settled in there. Amanda looked up at the darkness above the historical hotel. She hadn't agreed to come because she was desperate to see Santa arrive in Salem. It was just about spending time with family. Something inside her stirred, though. Her bear was feeling a tad off. She looked at the crowd around them. Most of them were families and couples, many dressed festively. All of them looked happy, or at the very worst, a little chilly. Why was her bear so restless?

"Isn't there just something about the holidays that makes you feel all cozy inside?" Tina said, rubbing her hands together and stomping her feet.

"Oh, definitely," Erin agreed, her face soft as she looked down at her son, whose eyes were glued to the fire truck. "I even like getting cold just so I can get warm again."

"It only feels that way because you've both found your mates," Kristy suggested. "The holidays for the rest of us are just a reminder that we haven't found ours yet."

"Don't think about it like that," Erin said, her eyes full of worry. "You still have plenty of family all around you."

But Kristy shook her head. "You wouldn't be saying that if you didn't have Jace! Family is great and all, and of course I love you guys, but it's just not the same. I'm fine the rest of the year, but then I have to watch all the couples giving each other gifts or kissing under the freaking mistletoe."

Tina, who had much more recently rediscovered her connection with her true mate, nodded. "You're right. The holidays can highlight all the things that have gone wrong, especially if it's been a minute since you've had…" She hesitated as she looked down at Sage, who was looking up at the hotel but still right there within earshot. "A good *meal*," she finally finished.

Erin let out a snort of laughter. "Maybe I am a little spoiled. I've been getting served plenty of good meals for a while now."

"Well-balanced ones," Kristy asked, her eyebrow arched, "or fast food?"

"If it's a busy week, sometimes you've just got to make sure you eat," Erin snickered. "Then on the weekends, you can have something that took a long time to cook, with premium ingredients."

"Shouldn't it be an all-you-can-eat buffet when you've always got someone to dine with?" Amanda asked.

All the women were laughing now. Fortunately, the kids seemed oblivious.

"You're lucky because you know exactly where to go when you're hungry," Kristy told Tina and Erin. "There are plenty of places to eat in the world, but you have to try them to see if you're going to like them. And most of them are pretty bad!"

"There should be a rating system," Amanda

suggested. "A place where you can just log in and find out if it's worth sitting down at the table or not."

Kristy was laughing so hard her eyes were watering now. "The last place I ate only served appetizers. No main course!"

Amanda braced herself on Kristy's arm as she wheezed. "At least you had that! It's been so long for me that I need a full Viking feast!"

As they cackled with laughter, a man standing in front of them turned around. His dark blond hair was carefully combed to the side and back, revealing a creased brow and piercing blue eyes. Those eyes looked straight into Amanda's as the corner of his mouth tipped up in amusement, accentuating his rugged, square jawline.

Her cheeks flushed with embarrassment, chasing away the chill of the night. Sage and Arden might not get the innuendo of their conversation, but that guy obviously did. She was still giggling a bit, but now she knew for sure that something was off with her bear. It lurched and pitched inside her. Thank goodness it was just some stranger. He might go home and tell his friends what he overheard in the crowd, but she'd never see him again.

"Hey, there's Chelsea!" Tina put her hand in the air and waved.

Chelsea, Beck, and Corbin saw them and made their way through the crowd. "We went ahead and got cocoa for Sage and Arden, too," Chelsea said, handing the drinks to each of the kids.

"Thank you!" Sage and Arden chorused.

"Ooh, marshmallows!" Sage added, poking one of them down with her finger so that it dunked into the hot liquid.

"I like eating all the marshmallows first," Corbin told them, showing them that his cup now had only cocoa in it.

"Did you lose your friend?" Erin asked.

"No, he's right here." Beck put his hand on the shoulder of the blonde man who'd turned and looked at Amanda a moment ago. "You guys came right to our spot without even trying!"

Oh, goddess. She just made a fool out of herself! The hot guy was a stranger to her, but not to Beck.

"This is Tina, Sage, Erin, Arden, Kristy, and Amanda," Beck said, making the introductions. "This is my old friend, Lars Olsen. He's here all the way from Longyearbyen."

Lars shook each of their hands, including those of the children.

"And where is that?" Erin asked.

"As far north as you can get," Lars replied, his accent pleasant. He reached for Amanda's hand.

It was more tempting to turn and run than to stay there, but what choice did she have? Darts of electricity pulsed up her arm from her palm as Lars took her hand. It felt like her magic flowing through her, but in reverse. "That's, uh, a very long way to come for Christmas," she managed.

His brow was heavy, making his gaze all the more intense. He was at least a head taller than Amanda, and the spice of his cologne reached her nose, even in the cold air. "I like to think it'll be worth it."

Beck beamed. "I thought it was time to show this old Viking what a Christmas in Salem is like."

Amanda's throat went tight. Couldn't she have picked some other way to talk about her dry spell?

But Lars had that impish smile on his face again.

"Look! Look!" Sage was pointing, jumping up and down.

They all turned as Santa himself appeared on the rooftop of the Hawthorne Hotel. He smiled and waved at the crowd below as the ladder from the fire truck slowly ascended to rescue him.

Now, if only *she* could be rescued.

The screams of the crowd around them intensified as all the children went nuts, impatient for

Santa to work his way down six stories' worth of ladder. The mob surged around them as the people in the back tried to get closer, jostling everyone forward. Tina, Erin, and Chelsea made sure the kids stayed in front of them, protected from the crush.

Amanda ended up standing directly next to Lars. She kept her gaze firmly locked on Santa, though every part of her body was highly aware of the handsome Norwegian. They were elbow to elbow, and she could feel the heat of his body through his sweater. Her heart thundered. She forced her lungs to slow down when she realized the visible steam from her breath was giving her away. Her bear was doing somersaults. Was she just embarrassed, or was this something more?

His arm slid against hers as he leaned over. "Where I'm from, Santa comes in the front door."

Surprised, she turned to him and found his face only a few inches away from hers. The crowd had pushed them even closer together than she'd realized. "Not down the chimney in the middle of the night?"

Again, he had that little smile on his face. "No, he's not that sneaky. He just comes right in the front door and gives you what you asked for."

This time, heat flushed through her entire body instead of just her face. "That's very bold of him."

"Just...honest." His eyes flicked down to her mouth, and then he returned to watching the spectacle.

When Santa was safely on the ground, much of the crowd began moving westward, where the Christmas tree would be lit in Lappin Park. "Are you ready to go?" Tina asked Sage.

"My feet hurt," she whined.

"Mine, too," Arden chimed in. He'd been attached to Sage ever since she'd first come to the Artemis Eclipse Sisterhood's covenstead, and it was quite possible he was only saying this for her sake.

"How about you?" Chelsea asked Corbin. "We could go watch the Christmas tree lighting, or we can get back to the house for the party."

"You should all join us," Beck suggested. "The kids can get comfortable and relax, and Lilith has really decked the place out. I think she's been cooking for the last few days."

"A party!" Sage's eyes lit up. "I like parties!"

"Me, too!" Arden echoed.

Erin smiled. "We'd love to come."

"Kristy? Amanda? You, too." Chelsea insisted.

Before she knew it, she was heading back to the Alexander clanhouse, hoping she didn't find any ways to embarrass herself more than she already had.

ALSO BY MEG RIPLEY
ALL AVAILABLE ON AMAZON

Shifter Nation Universe

Enchanted Over Forty Series

Destined Over Forty Series

Marked Over Forty Series

Fated Over Forty Series

Mates Under the Mistletoe: A Shifter Nation Christmas Collection

Wild Frontier Shifters Series

Special Ops Shifters: L.A. Force Series

Special Ops Shifters: Dallas Force Series

Special Ops Shifters Series (original D.C. Force)

Werebears of Acadia Series

Werebears of the Everglades Series

Werebears of Glacier Bay Series

Werebears of Big Bend Series

Dragons of Charok Universe

Daddy Dragon Guardians Series

Shifters Between Worlds Series

Dragon Mates: The Complete Dragons of Charok Universe Collection (Includes Daddy Dragon Guardians and Shifters Between Worlds)

More Shifter Romance Series

Beverly Hills Dragons Series

Dragons of Sin City Series

Dragons of the Darkblood Secret Society Series

Packs of the Pacific Northwest Series

Compilations

Forever Fated Mates Collection

Shifter Daddies Collection

Early Novellas

Mated By The Dragon Boss

Claimed By The Werebears of Green Tree

Bearer of Secrets

Rogue Wolf

ABOUT THE AUTHOR

Steamy shifter romance author Meg Ripley is a Seattle native who's relocated to New England. She can often be found whipping up her next tale curled up in a local coffee house with a cappuccino and her laptop.

Download *Alpha's Midlife Baby,* the steamy prequel to Meg's Fated Over Forty series, when you sign up for the Meg Ripley Insiders newsletter!

Sign up by visiting www.authormegripley.com

Connect with Meg

amazon.com/Meg-Ripley/e/B00Z8I9AXW
tiktok.com/@authormegripley
facebook.com/authormegripley
instagram.com/megripleybooks
bookbub.com/authors/meg-ripley
goodreads.com/megripley
pinterest.com/authormegripley

Printed in Dunstable, United Kingdom